Sweet union since ancient times
Gets poets in-between connected:
They are the priests of single muse,
To single flame they are affected

Puskin A.S.

For senior school age

Goethe and Abai

Herold Belger Essay

Hertfordshire Press
London 2015

Published in United Kingdom
Hertfordshire Press Ltd © 2015

9 Cherry Bank, Chapel Street
Hemel Hempstead, Herts.
HP2 5DE, United Kingdom

e-mail: publisher@hertfordshirepress.com
www.hertfordshirepress.com

GOETHE AND Abai
Herold Belger Essay

English

Edited by David Parry
Cover design by Aleksandra Vlasova
Typesetting All Well Solutions,
Assistant: Akylai Akirova

*Published by the support of the
Embassy of the Republic of Kazakhstan
to the United Kingdom*

---

*British Library Catalogue in Publication Data
A catalogue record for this book is available from the British Library
Library of Congress in Publication Data
A catalogue record for this book has been requested*

ISBN 978-1-910886-16-8

Printed by Mega Printing in Turkey

CONTENTS

INTRODUCING SPIRITUAL TWINS

As something of a diehard Jungian, I have recently developed an interest in Astrology. A fascination partly evolving from the fact this antique science once studied wandering planets with an attitude akin to documenting the movements of vagrants, prodigies, nomads, anomalies, and pilgrims. A pursuit with clearly explanatory, even if not always causal, depths. Maybe my current obsession also arose because this arcane pursuit revealed previously covert connections between people, places and events. Promising, thereby, to elucidate seamless patterns, which would otherwise remain inexplicable. Particularly when considering similar types of genius in far distant lands, or betwixt obvious spiritual twins – men related by outlook, creativity, and a general sense of humanitarianism – even if not by tribal heritage.

Of course, Britain is a nation of wanderers, prodigies and travellers. We journey here, We voyage there. Indeed, we Brits cannot really rest unless we are examining the world around us. Exploring the miracles of Great Nature Herself, or noting the environmental wonders experienced by fantastical peoples in faraway lands. And as someone hailing from a "small island" (as the American author Bill Bryson humorously phrases it), or dreaming of Grand Tours away from misty Albion (as natives tend to envisage things), I am convinced we Islanders are blessed with a series of uncommon sensibilities. In a way, our meanderings permit us to scrutinize the usually overlooked. The abstract, imaginal distinctions, for instance, between being landlocked, or surrounded by the sea. Certainly, as a poet, I find myself weirdly sensitised to the timelessly tense, yet youthfully intrepid, energy of Kazakhstan. A threefold irony, when bearing in mind the sheer cultural age of these hallowed geographies! Moreover, the lovely city of Almaty seems to embody a settled metropolis, although, underneath, there is a pulse of surging (contemporary) nomadism akin to the compulsions experienced by ancient wanderers from the sacred Steppes. Unsurprising, possibly, when considering Central Asia as a whole, rather like Almaty, appears to be in unending process. Eurocentric scholars, no doubt, tend to resist such "private" perceptions in their brutish descriptions of these mighty territories: bounded, as these lands are, by the Caspian Sea to the west, and to the east by the Tarim Basin. Never forgetting entire geoscapes rimmed in the south by the Amu Darya (Oxus River). All meaning, probably, that in real terms such professors shamelessly ignore impressions delineating Tibet as mystical, Mongolia as lusty, Turkmenistan as vigorous, Uzbekistan as exotic, and Azerbaijan as delightfully sensuous. Or for that matter, Afghanistan as impenetrable, Nepal as magical, Bhutan as legendary, as well as parts of Mother Russia as Holy. Each a complex aesthetic location in its own right, and helping to explain why respected Western critics, if not academicians, share my own sense of literary befuddlement. Due, in no reduced part, to the fact such rich textual forms - along with obviously sophisticated lyrical content - were expressed a myriad of tongues, scripts, and alphabets. Often defiant, in themselves, of any given analysis.

1. From the 17th to the 20th century

So stated, I need to make a contextualizing confession. Central Asian literatures, expressed through such vibrant cultures, have long been a fascination of mine. Looking back, I am not sure there is any logical explanation for this preoccupation, but it is, nonetheless, a personal truth. A near obsession, dare I say, starting with Russian novels when I was a teenager, and eventually evolving into an irresistible attraction towards the verse, folktales, and drama of distant Central Asian demes. Especially, in my case, Turkic-inspired literatures! Undoubtedly, the lush depths of these sumptuous (even though profoundly spiritual) texts enthralled me. The rarefied delicacies of insight, accompanied as they invariably were by a robust understanding of psychology, drew me with an almost magnetic charm. Thus, I mentally travelled through the thought-worlds of a number of these literatures. Noticing, by the 17th century, they had achieved luxurious heights unsuspected by our Western commentators of the day. Culminating, debatably, in the 18th century, when the poetry of Makhtumquli reached its exuberant zenith. Acknowledged so, Turkmen literature remained highly influential across vast regions of Central Asia until the later 19th century, when sturdy Kazakh voices were finally heard above competing textual traditions. In a manner, strangely reminiscent of British authors in times past. Unarguably, if I remind myself of those days when I started to investigate such puzzling poetic phenomena - and fully realizing the Kazakhs lacked a unified state in that period – these gallant, albeit wilful, literary wonderers supported a flourishing oral literature. Creating classic forms, if one wishes to express it so, recited by professional bards similar to our European troubadours. Further, I observed that by the 19th century, the Kyrgyz had collected a vast oral literature around their national hero Manas, whilst the Uzbek tribes under Turkmen influence, evolved their own epics (known as *destān*), which strongly reminded me of the poetic cycles surrounding King Arthur and his Knights of the Round Table. Yet, these striking correspondences seem to have ended once Russian political hegemony became dominant in this region. Meaning, somewhat unexpectedly, I had come full circle and returned to my interest in Russian literature from another angle. Unlike, my small Island home, therefore, the 19th century in Central Asia witnessed emergent transitional literatures within which inherited literary practices gave way to modern transnational genres: especially among the Kazakhs. For example, the second half of this century saw the great Abai Qunanbaev (Abai Ibrahim Kūnanbay-ulï) fuse native Kazakh with Russian literary themes. Elsewhere, even though a little later, Soviet influences engendered openly Modernist literatures reaching fruition in the 20th century with Abdullah Qadiriy's first successful novels in Uzbek, whilst Mukhtar Auez-ulï simultaneously became an outstanding contemporary writer in the Kazakh tongue. Undeniably, the Russian language acting as a worthy catalyst for these innovations. Leading, that stressed, pundits to claim the greatest exemplification of this textual fusion was to be found in the works of Kyrgyz novelist Chingiz Aitmatov: a 20th-century Central Asian author who wrote predominantly in Russian.

2. Man on the Way

Be that as critical comment may, my intuitions still suspect there is a subtle, although ultimately fundamental, creative distinction between the literatures of wanderers and those of travellers. Primarily because, at the end of the day, a traveller wishes to return home to recount his, or her, adventures, whereas wanderers embody a healthy devil-may-care attitude towards life generally: and may choose to settle wherever the Divine Muse takes them. Sympathetic to such dual inklings, the German novelist Thomas Mann (1875-1955), allows Hans Castorp (the protagonist) in his masterful novel The Magic Mountain to confess his fixation with the elusive Clavdia Chauchat due, in large part, to the enigma posed by her Kyrgyz eyes. A recurrent motif, curiously, throughout the narrative, since "Kyrgyz eyes" were also a feature of Castorp's earlier, breathless, infatuation with a young boy who many years previously had loaned him a pencil in his school playground. Each of these episodes manifestly alluding to the wildly erotic, even though strikingly alien, attractions associated with such features in our Western European psyches. Atop this, one of Castorp's two main mentors, the rationalist Ludovico Settembrini, openly confesses his inward fears regarding "nomadic inclinations" along the Silk Road. A totally unexpected reaction from a man who prides himself on an attitude of optimistic progressivism for all of humankind. Unforgettably then, this demanding book blends a scrupulous realism with primal, symbolic, undertones, in its attempt to raise questions concerning the impetus of literature itself. An enterprise, which inspired me to reflect that travellers tend to write detailed "snapshots" of phenomena. So, in the manner of "serious" tourists, they collect and comment upon every single phenomena our planet has to offer their investigations. By contrast, the literature of wonderers is more like a map. Authors joining dots and finding links between topographies otherwise inexplicable to their readers. It goes without saying, this discerned, such views are personal, as well as theoretical works in progress.

Nevertheless, as a pertinent case in point, the recent novel by Abdulla Isa (AKA Zaur Hasanov) entitled Man of the Mountains seems to verify these conjectures. Beyond question, Hasanov as a writer ascends truly classical plateaus of literary attainment within Western aesthetic convention. Furthermore, his impressive first person narrative will immediately catch any Anglo-American reader's eye due to the strength of its "highland" characters. All be they within harsh, yet dynamic, Chechen social structures. Yet, in this engaging tale of lost innocence and radicalization, it is the terrain itself, which acts as the true protagonist. Above inquiry, these living, rugged, landscapes gift

Hasanov's "hero" (also known as Zaur), with an unending courage, as well as a naive foolhardiness. Psychological features said to be typical of those who mature amid titanic panoramas and, possibly, the hallmarks of any text detailing the progressions of homo viator, or "Man on the Way" to borrow a phrase from theology. Thenceforth, this book is worthy of a large international readership, because it equally raises issues regarding differing frames of genre-intention.

Another striking illustration of a ceaselessly questing literature is The Silent Steppe: the Memoir of a Kazakh Nomad by Mukhamet Shayakhmetov. Born to a slightly earlier generation than Hasanov, this author lived through the rigours of experimental collectivisation, famine, and the violent horrors of Stalingrad. Tortuous experiences undoubtedly explaining why this book was slow in reaching readerships in either America, or Britain. Disgracefully, it took five decades before it was stacked on our bookshelves because certain "enlightened" critics refused to admit the grim realities behind gulag-inspired autobiographies, or the medical incarceration of dissidents. Nonetheless, Shayakhmetov's account of his Fate (the original title) is worth a hundred endnotes written by historians. Assuredly, on reflection, it is the physical settings which prove radical for western tastes, since they contain detailed ethnographies, nomadic practices and local customs, blended with chapters wherein he describes how (as a nine-year-old boy), he roamed alone in search of lodgings: almost in the style of a survival guide for living on the steppe. Inherited clan systems, according to Shayakhmetov, being best understood as a source of corruption in Central Asian politics, although the only guarantee of survival in such conditions. Undeniably, their disassembling reads like a Greek tragedy! In addition, by illuminating a Central Asian version of Islam, Shayakhmetov draws memorable portraits of friends and family alike (Russian and Kazakh), to preserve them against impersonal historical processes. Now a retired headmaster (we are told), living in west Kazakhstan, he explains that he wrote his book for modern generations of Kazakhs. To show them, as it were, how their grandparents lived. Anyway, it has a great deal to teach us foreigners too, respecting a dignified life-affirming endurance while in the midst of palpable suffering.

Powerfully allied to this, Nemat Kelimbatov's heartrending I Don't Want To Lose Hope traces the cartography of faith-against-circumstance in a manifestly autobiographical tour de force. To my mind, mapping interior states of fortitude as ingeniously as any imaginative adventurer describes wandering across the rolling countryside. Arguably a recurrent fixation in the arts of this region, Kelimbatov stuns his readers by outlining ten years of actual bedridden paralysis (following an operation on his spine), thereby unwrapping his journey into perpetual struggle. What is more, by comparing, his hospital to a grave wherein he was buried alive, he tells the type of tale which guides both his characters, as well as his readers, into greater levels of spiritual orientation and transcendent value. All in all, a challenging, unique, text, narrating the lonely realities only a wanderer in these moral wastes could ever truly understand. An astonishing existential achievement!

3. Conclusion

Analysed so, what does all this mean in terms of Herold Belger's extended essay on Goethe and Abai? Well, as a diehard Jungian who remains aware that men once watched the skies to become healthy, wealthy, and discern otherwise hidden connections, a great deal. In this genuinely ingenious work, Belger has hit on a profound acausal link between genius in the Weimar Republic and creativity on the Steppes. As such, he has grasped that Goethe and Abai are spiritual twins. Brothers beneath the skin. Astral family, as it were, as well as two of the originators of World Literature. Put differently, the work of Goethe and Abai, once interpreted correctly, allows us to realise Western European literary endeavours were echoed across Central Asia. Today, this acknowledged, epithets like "Global Text" designate the continuing circulation of these materials into a wider dispersal than an author's mere country of origin. Hence, since the mid-1990's lively debate, both outside and within academia, about the spiritual, political, and aesthetic, value of this Great Work has emerged. From my side, I am proud to recall English literature has frequently been named as the "Second Great Tradition", a title fully deserved because it embodies a continuous stream of poems, dramas and novels preserving vital reflections on our human condition. As for Central Asian literature, I, personally, have never found it wanting. Or for that matter struggling to come up to the attainments of the West. It is apposite to say Central Asia needs more voices expressing themselves on the world stage in order to start reaching the sheer textual output of European corpuses, yet the quality of authors from these regions already speaks for itself. After all these centuries, therefore, Abai is still very much the equal brother of Goethe. In which case, these spiritual twins remind us that literature does not simply describe our specific environment, or carefully detail the minutiae of clashing psychologies around us. Rather, our world is mapped, photographed, and at the same time transcended by its employment. All of which, thanks to Belger, posits an extraordinarily important, albeit different, angle to global literature as an entirety.

David Parry
London 2015

REVIEWS

"to perceive through the heart, through the soul"
Herold Belger

Devotees of both Abai Kunanbayev and Johann Wolfgang von Goethe will surely welcome Herfordshire Press's present publication of Herold Belger's personal and scholarly essay on these two giants of world literature. Belger's unique stance is to follow the dictates of his imagination, inspired by a close life-long study of Goethe and Abai, and, alongside many detailed scholarly investigations, e.g. his comparative study of Goethe and Abai's innovations in poetic metre, form and consonance, or of the sources and background of Goethe's Eastern inspired masterpiece *West-East Divan*, Belger muses openly about the personal impact that Goethe and Abai have had on him. From the start, Belger makes it plain that he does not set out to "compare or oppose these giants" and anyway, "there is no question of direct influence in this case - nevertheless, one can hint about a philosophical and aesthetic harmony amongst these two spiritual giants." Inevitably then, this essay is both a record of Belger's long personal fascination with Goethe and Abai, and of the elevated inspiration they provide for heartfelt reflections on the art of living in general. These two poets are not to sit on the dusty shelves of a library; rather, by bringing them to life, Belger invites us to share in his enthusiasm and maybe become inspired to build on their achievements in our present age.

I will leave Belger to introduce these two great men to you in his own way, however, for Western readers unfamiliar with Abai Ibrahim Kunanbayev — for whom Belger's essay might provide a most welcome and engaging first introduction — it is as well to appreciate that Abai has for long been a figure of well-deserved national veneration in Kazakhstan. He lived from 1845 to 1904, in an era of instability and confusion for the Kazakh people and came to represent a much needed unifying, national voice for moral, spiritual and political regeneration.

His voice continues to speak with ringing authority for the Kazakh people to this day.

Belger's sustained and personal reverence for his fellow Kazakh, the great poet Abai is naturally strong, as it is similarly for Muktar Auezov: 'Abai is a deep river. I only draw from it with a ladle'. Part of Belger's intention then is, at least, to reveal to his readers the many facets of Abai's rich poetic output, burnished in the heat of what he estimates to be the comparable fire of Goethe's (possibly greater) accomplishments more familiar to Western readers.

In general terms then, for Belger, as one might for instance deduce from his comments on Goethe's *West-östlicher Diwan* (1819): "West-East Divan reveals a catechism to life affirming spiritual humanism which is Goethe's credo." For both Goethe and Abai then, Belger identifies 'life affirming spiritual humanism' as the one great overarching theme, allied in both men's cases to a deep sense of engagement in the wider community of 'world literature'. One by one and at length and in detail, Belger discourses on the many common, underlying strands which he identifies in their great personal and cultural endeavours; these are all themes that have long fascinated him. For both poets he sees these themes as providing the rich field of expression for their personal affirmations of life: first perhaps Nature — and it is especially delightful to become acquainted with some of Abai's celebrated depictions of vernacular life in the awesome natural setting of the Kazakh Steppe — also love, music, the nobility of the poet's mission, the difficulty of poetry, personal effort and loss, painful experiences of betrayal and incomprehension, the exercise of political office, the tragic loss of their own children, was well as broader socio-cultural issues of national unity and the more artistic project of poetic and linguistic reform. The reform of the language itself also embraces a cultural mission, namely to create a truly national literary language. Notwithstanding the widely separated cultural milieus of Goethe and Abai, which both poets illustrate so graphically and realistically in their work, Belger takes his reader on an intense journey through his common thematic landscape, a landscape of the imagination which transcends East and West.

Belger's discussion of Goethe's *West-East Divan* — a set of poems apparently deeply controversial in their day — is fascinatingly informative in itself. I would note in passing, for Western readers, that 'divan' in this context refers to a conversation or meeting place, by metaphorical extension then, to a cultural bridge between Asia and the West. This relates to a personal interest of my own in Belger's text at this point: as producer for Orzu Arts, Britain's only Central Asian theatre and arts company, I have since 2012 been involved in presenting performances of Ovlyakuli Khodjakuli's one-man play *Mejnun*, directed and acted by Orzu Arts' founder Yuldosh Juraboev. Khodjakuli's *Mejnun* dramatises large sections of Goethe's *Divan*, as well as the Central Asian legends of Sheikh Sanan and Leyli and Mejnun. In presenting such a work on modern world stages, at the Edinburgh International Festival, also in London, Kyrgyzstan and Uzbekistan etc., we have inevitably been engaging with precisely the same issues in the 21st century as Goethe and Abai did poetically in the nineteenth. There is no end to the lessons that love can teach us.

Ever since Marco Polo's famous and colourful eye witness accounts of his travels along the Silk Roads to China first reached Europe, in which the 13th century Venetian merchant also brought the legendary Kublai Khan and the Steppes of Asia so vividly to life, this region has preserved an almost magical fascination for Westerners. Goethe was certainly in its thrall, a fact which is surprisingly little discussed in the West. I was therefore particularly interested to learn from Belger that Goethe, who had first encountered the poetry of Hafiz around 1814, was working on an unfinished drama *Mohammed* when he died. If Abai maintained a keen and thoughtful lifelong self-education in the literature and philosophy of the Western world, as Belger describes, conversely, Goethe had a similarly prolonged fascination and intimate knowledge of the great Eastern art and thought traditions, including the poetry of such as Rumi, Hafiz, Ferdosi, Navai etc. This I have found inspiring for my own, present cultural projects.

Belger: 'it is easy to imagine what attracted Goethe to the poetry of the East. The versified brilliance, sensuality and freedom, high spirituality, a charm for the world, harmony of the Spirit and the Word, the ardour of imagination, joyous, elegant expressiveness, allied to an allegorical way of thinking and so on.

To the purer East then, fly
Patriarchal air to try:
Loving, drinking, songs among,
Khizer's rill will make you young.'

By a stroke of coincidence, Belger — who himself delights in coincidences of this sort — is here citing precisely the opening lines of Khodjakuli's *Mejnun*, a new play which also explores the profound and, it is important to bear in mind, perennial theme of the cultural land-bridge between Europe and Central Asia. Belger again: 'unsurprisingly then, the theme of love in the 'West-East Divan' is permeated by Eastern philosophy, Eastern attitudes, Eastern tradition, and Eastern forms of expression.' Conveying these to modern audiences is a taxing, and we at Orzu Arts believe, also profoundly valuable proposition. Belger discusses the manner in which Abai and Goethe saw the social expression of love: as a sincere sharing of the heart. 'Numerous variations of the "heart" theme, the multi-valued image of the "heart" as a vessel of spiritual substance, along with the cult of the heart — are significant motifs within Goethe and Abai. To my mind, a traditional style used by Eastern poets. A device, moreover, joyfully employed by Goethe on numerous occasions.'

Engaging with the social dynamics of love relations on stage is also a central theme not only of Orzu's *Mejnun,* but also of our more recent productions of contemporary Kazakh author Dulat Issabekov's *Transit Passenger.* Our British actors Kathy Trevelyan and Mark Stanton had to work long and hard at developing a sensibility for the psycho-physcial attitudes of the play's two central Kazakh characters, not least to learn how Central Asians conduct their love relations. This personal exploration they both had to make in order to be able to present the Kazakh couple's transient experience of intimacy authentically on stage, and hence make it believable to audiences in both London and Astana. For our two British actors, this was a tough and rewarding imaginative journey: thus, Juraboev's creative process of directing the rehearsal process of Issabekov's *Transit Passenger,* involved taking two Europeans on the very same cross-cultural journey Goethe had been so eloquently describing in *West-East Divan,* albeit transposed into a world 200 hundred years later. There is a powerful message here for our conflict ridden age.

My second personal interest in Abai is in the musical aspects of his output, and I was captivated reading Belger's own stories of hearing Abai's music being performed. As a performing classical musician myself, as well as teacher at the Guildhall School of Music and Goldsmith Colleges in London, I found these glimpses of Abai the composer enticing, enticing I say because his music is so little known in the West. I managed to find only a few short clips of musical performances of his haunting vocal melodies available on the internet. As part of my own work, I am particularly interested in the issue of narrative in music (especially instrumental music), and am currently engaged in studying Mozart's masterly 1785 musicalisation, KV.476, of Goethe's beautiful narrative poem *Das Veilchen*. Goethe famously decried composers (Franz Schubert for example) setting his work to music, presumably judging that his poems should best be permitted to speak for themselves. From Belger's essay it appears that this was very much not the case with Abai. I would therefore love to hear more of how Abai manages to project his narrative poetic concerns into the world of sung and instrumental music. Belger mentions Zhubanov, for example, for whom 'Abai's songs were written not by an illustrator, but by a composer. They feature musical qualities and played a major role in the development of musical culture amongst the Kazakh people.' It would be good to hear more about Abai's important role as a musical catalyst in Kazakhstan. Another question I have is whether printed study scores of Abai's music are available. Belger also mentions the musicologist A.V.Zataevich's '1000 Songs of the Kazakh People' (1925). This would no doubt be another rich, secondary source of further material for musical research in the same vein. Additionally, on the subject of primary sources, I would be intrigued to hear of any further ethnomusicological searches done in Kazakhstan, or indeed more widely in Central Asia, of the sort undertaken by Cecil Sharpe and Ralph Vaughan-Williams in Britain and by Zoltan Kodaly and Bela Bartok in the Hungarian regions during the first half of the 20th century. It seems to me that Abai might stand as the patron saint of such endeavour in Kazakhstan. His own musical aims were closely bound to his political aims of a peaceful unification of the Kazakh people. Seeking to celebrate the art of great poet-musicians of the Kazakh oral traditions, Abai it seems wrote Kazakh folk-style music for performances of his own poetry. His practice harks back at least 4000 years to regional traditions of reciting the vast and ancient tale of Manas in musicalised song.

The United Nations' Educational, Scientific and Cultural Organisation declared 1995 the Year of Abai. On this occasion, the President of the Republic of Kazakhstan, N. Nazarbayev gave a long address, describing, among other things, the difficult and turbulent political circumstances in which Abai lived and his important role in helping his country to rise above them:

'The magnificence of Abai's genius lies in the fact that in an epoch of colonial oppression and humiliation he managed — contrary to all vicissitudes — to ennoble the fortitude of the Kazakh national spirit, instilling persistence and daring rather than wary cowardice, purposefulness rather than confusion, a striving to knowledge rather than ignorance and career-seeking into the minds of his fellow-tribesmen'.

The President concluded by praising Abai as a national hero, a status extended internationally on this occasion by UNESCO. It would seem that Abai's humanistic call for ethnic unity and social concord, for political, cultural and moral renewal through general education are all endeavours for which Kazakhstan, in 2015, is now so much better placed than in his own day.

I would like to conclude with some final words on what I see as the crucial matter of translation. Firstly, I cannot commend highly enough the excellent work of David Parry and of Marat Akhmedjanov's hard working editorial team at Hertfordshire Press in preparing this final version of Belger's essay in English. I have a keen sense that it is translation, at its many levels, which is the essential and yet somewhat unsung enabler and key to the great cross-cultural entreprise of which publishing Herold Belger's essay on Abai and Goethe is part. Translation certainly was vital for Abai himself, assiduously accessing as he did the world's literature and philosophy in translations, by Lermontov and others.

Belger himself already regrets 'so many losses when translating Abai into Russian'. So much more then, must any further rendition into English be accomplished with linguistic skill, artistic sensitivity and intelligence. In fact this is *sine qua non*, if the riches of the Central

Asian arts, Abai included, are to become more fully appreciated in the West. Close attention to this core issue is beautifully reflected in the elegant success, with which the volume you now hold in your hands not only captures Belger's views, but also provides a clear and precious glimpse of the guiding genius of the two poets he so revered, Goethe and Abai.

By Joseph Sanders
MA Cantab, ARAM, Dip.RAM
London, 15 October 2015
2330 Words

Joseph Sanders read Modern Languages at Cambridge University before setting out on a freelance career as a concert oboist. Since 2008 he is a regular guest with London Symphony Orchestra and other leading ensembles. Prior to that he dedicated himself to classical contemporary music performance. He is member of the teaching staff at The Guildhall School of Music and Drama and Goldsmith's College in London, with whom he has been involved in music performance research. He also teaches the Alexander Technique.

REVIEWS

Abai (Ibrahim) Qunanbayuli and Johann Wolfgang Goethe are two people from different ages that actually come together through radical thinking. Their sole aim through their individual writings was to open the minds of nations to unite in understanding of each other.

It would seem that Goethe could not settle on one path in life, however his contribution to society was immense. He wanted justice for all and studied law and is enthusiasm resulted in a failure at the first attempt, only to take up the career at a later date. His time in Italy had a great influence on him.

His writings and poetry transcended the divisions between the written word and music with composers, including *Wolfgang Amadeus Mozart, Ludwig van Beethoven, Franz Schubert, Robert Schumann, Johannes Brahms, Charles Gounod, Richard Wagner, Hugo Wolf, Felix Mendelssohn, Hector Berlioz, Gustav Mahler*, and *Jules Massenet* putting his work to music.

Abai's contribution to Central Asia is to show the world that different cultures are connected through showing ideology is not far removed from anywhere in Europe and Central Asia. For Abai to be acknowledged in Moscow a city that fights between Western outlook on life and Asian values is a great mark of the influence he had on the cultural values of his time.

I have no doubt if Abai and Goethe were alive at the same time, their joint influence would have had a great influence on bringing Central Asia and Western Europe together much quicker.

It is now that with like minded people we can unite two great areas of the world together respecting each other's cultures and values.

Alan Cox
Staffordshire England

Alan Cox is a world renowned psychic consultant, healer and psychic surgeon. He is also an accomplished radio broadcaster hosting three radio shows. These shows are internet based and listened to all over the world with huge following. They are "Understanding Spirit", "Musical Memories" and "Inspirational Voices" all on www.paramaniaradio.com. Inspirational voices is co hosted with Jillian Haslam and brings to the airways people from all walks of life from all over the world who have overcome major adversity in their life.

REVIEWS

Two star'o'souls

As a new age author I got the honorable task of writing about Ibrahim "Abai" Qunanbaiuli and Johann wolfgang von Goethe. In realizing the common ground we share in some of our basic convictions, they are worthy champions who deserve to be acknowledged more than I ever could do justice. Both were fighters for mutual enrichment of their fellow humans as they had to live their own lives. Goethe was a poet, statesman and scientist, he was a botanist. Abai was a poet, composer and philosopher. While Goethe went into Sturm und Drang and wrote his fameous book. Abai was busy translating old works into Khazakh, and implementing social changes, among the works abai translated was the works of Goethe. They were fighting souls seperated by the machination of time and geography. Goethe was german born in 1749 while Abai was born in Khazakztan in the year of 1845. Abai died at the age of 58 while Goethe lived to be 82.

Not much in the Europe is known about Abai but more is known in Russia and Khazakstan. Akin to Goethe Abai experienced wars in his time, and they were both marked by this. They didnt live under the same conditions; whilst Goethe were born to a prominent well off family, the more humble origins of Abai only made him able to attend to a russian school. And while Goethe experienced the french revolution, Abai was born over a century after Goethe died. Considering the history of both men seperated by over a century, Goethe was perhaps a bit more "visible" than Abai considering their diverse backgrounds, but maybe not more important. While Goethe enjoyed a profiled life where he had the possibility of distancing himself into alltogether philosophical perspectives, Abai were more earthbound into real political and sociological changes in his milue. One can only speculate what either of the men really thought when seeing wars and social conflicts in their time. Both being poets and philosophers, the wrath cursing their veins at social injustice. The questions arise amidst the praise any person of the people deserve. They were both interested in the enrichment of those around them.

Goethe became one of the influences to Abai It is therefore quite plausible to claim they were both concerned about Europe. Europe at both the mens living time was ravaged by conflict and change. Is it possible to see how this influenced them? What was their sense of injustise? These were revolutionary men of their time, becuase they have lived through wars or becuase they could sense it was all avoidable somehow. Surely neither of them could ignore the signs in history. As Goethe and "Abai" eventually had to give in to time after all they had been alive for, did they feel disapointed or satisfied?

Both Goethe and Abai deserve to be re-examined, becuase even if the men fought all their life, their works include great beauty and holds drama, sharing in the world of arts.

By Johan alstad
Written 11.10.2015

New age author and lecturer Johan alstad specialises in subtle energies and mystical lore.
34 years old and thirsty for knowledge he is restless in challenging himself in search for all kinds of knowledge.
Has self-published 5 books. 3 books on amazon. 1 booklet with essays in Amerika under the pseudonyme Trax chaos. 1 book in his home country Norway with both poems and small essays.
The books on amazon is published under the name Johan alstad.

REVIEWS

There is a tendency amongst the Anglo-American peoples to overlook what lies beyond the invisible boundaries of Western literature, resulting in what essentially is an ignorance of countless, but also, magnificent works of art in the non-western world. Undoubtedly, The Central Asian country of Kazakhstan is one that has given rise to many historically significant producers of art. As the founder of modern Kazakh literature, Abai Kunanbaev (1845-1904) is, indeed, one of the most renowned Kazakh 'artists' of his era who fundamentally transformed the cultural aspects of Kazakh nation through his innovative writings. He not only translated the works of Western and Russian giants like Goethe and Pushkin, but also merged together Western philosophical and artistic values with those of enlightened Islam in his poetry.

Indeed, upon a closer look, one may find that there are parallel patterns of creative imagination and philosophical thought between Abai and his European counterpart. A notable example can be seen between Goethe's Faust and Abai's the Book of Words. Faust, the protagonist of Goethe's tragic play, is a scholar and an alchemist who is confronted by an incomplete satisfaction with the limitations extreme rationalism. Subsequently, he feels spirituality and fusion of life with nature and universe will complete him. Similarly, in his Book of Words, Abai ponders on the possible paths that he may follow after a lifetime of gaining knowledge, whereupon he, ultimately, decides that the only way for him is to follow the way of an artist through 'pen and paper'.

Similarly, both Abai and Goethe were critiques of their era: Abai condemned the illiteracy prevalent amongst the Kazakh people, while Goethe condemned the extreme rationalism of the Enlightenment era. Abai's and Goethe's works showed their belief that human life could not be satisfied through reason alone, that, instead, art and emotion were fundamental in making it whole. Indeed, although at the time, Kazakhstan and Europe were materially different than each other,

Abai promoted not only the Enlightenment values of rationalism, education and science, but he also promoted arts and spirituality to the Kazakh people as the way for the improvement of Kazakhstan as a nation.

Undoubtedly, Kazakhstan's great feats of progress that have been achieved since the twentieth century owes much to Abai's genius as an artist. Both Goethe and Abai contributed, in similar ways, to what essentially was lacking from their respective societies. Germany lacked the essential values of Romanticism, Kazakhstan lacked literacy and education. By harnessing the works of European giants and many other cultures, Abai transformed the written literature of Kazakhstan. Art, however, was essential to him as he was aware of the dangers of extreme rationalism. Indeed, all of this demonstrates that a link exists between Central Asia and Europe in ways that are essentially cultural and historical, and therefore, points to a crucial need for an open dialogue between the two cultures.

Daniele H. Irandoost
Aberystwyth 2015

As an undergraduate student from the Aberystwyth University, I pursue a degree in International Politics and Intelligence Studies. My interests, however, are not restricted to the study of politics in the international stage, or for that matter the study of intelligence. Indeed, on many occasions I have endeavoured to broaden my knowledge of world literature, pursuing, for instance, a deeper understanding of gigantic artists like Dostoyevsky, Hemmingway, Goethe, and even the Persian Poet Ferdowsi amongst others. That being said, my fascination with literature does not end on a personal level. Upon my arrival to Britain from Iran, I participated in poetry events in London (Poetry Café) and Aberystwyth (Arts Centre), whereupon I attempted to familiarise the western audience with translations of Persian poetry. Additionally, in one poetry event, called 'Homage to Shelly', at the Aberystwyth Arts Centre, I was fortunate enough to perform the role of Shelly Bysshe, the writer of the political poem, *the Mask of Anarchy*. Overall, as an internationally inclined student, I find the pursuit of an open dialogue in culture and literature between the nations of the West and the East not only beneficial to myself but also essential to the advancement of humanity in general.

Daniele H. Irandoost
Aberystwyth 2015

Goethe
and
Abai

Herold Belger Essay

Reviewer Plashevsky Y.P.
member of the USSR Writers Union

GOETHE AND ABAI

Let your inquisitive eye
Tirelessly watch the creative flow,
Join the earth's chosen ones.

Goethe.

To see the torch of truth —
One should have a sighted heart.

Abai.

So strange: it seems to me that I feel Abai.

I believe that feeling someone else's work is, beyond doubt, more dimensional and significant than understanding. Normal people are able to understand, to comprehend many things. But to feel, that is to perceive through the heart, through the soul – is very difficult. It is like love, like a gift: you either have it, or not.

The song sung from the heart,
Owns the poet's soul and heart.

states Goethe in his poem "Confession".
The same was said by Abai:

Word, comprehended by brain,
As empty sound sleeps away.
But fire fills your vein,
If your soul takes it to stay.
                    (translation into Russian by Rozhdestvenskiy Vs.

But Abai in the original used the expression "diligent heart" («ынталы жүрек») » instead of "soul" – Yet, the word, comprehended by a diligent heart, is effectively the same.

Obviously is no coincidence that one of the most frequent phrases in the poetry of Goethe is "das Herz" - heart with all the endless nuances of its meaning. And, of course, it is no coincidence "the heart", *жүрек*, - is a, comprehensive image in the workings of Abai. How many times he falls back upon it, and how many definitions he finds for it!

All meaning, some may think my way to Abai through Goethe is obscure? After all, I'm German, though I was brought up in a Kazakh aul[1]. Yet, this is not the case. In actuality, it is Goethe I've been stealthily approaching across the years through Abai. Certainly, such confessions may seem odd at first sight. Especially when recalling my examination of Goethe's "Night Song of the Wanderer" - which I studied in the light of Abai's *«Қараңғы түнде тау қалғып»* (through "Mountain Peaks" by Lermontov) took such an indirect route. In other words, my circuitous path was inverse – from creek to headspace.

Well… the ways of knowledge are bizarre and mysterious.

The last thing I'd like to disclose is my attraction to the characters of these people, even though, of course, I do not consider myself an Abai, or Goethe connoisseur. However, the unquestionable and doubtless affinity of muses shared by these men, along with their obvious spiritual similarities is clearly uncanny. Hence, it is strange to say this theme – Goethe and Abai, has not been addressed before, even though the hallmarks connecting them are transparent. A bonding, dare I suggest, made since my student years (sometimes very obscure and sometimes transparent), wherein I sensed a consonance betwixt these two great men. From that time onwards, I could identify and express this apparent unity. I found it in the identity between coincidental ideas and thoughts, as well as in stylistic resonances inside some verse lines. All marking an affinity of psychophysical natures in these two Poets. Along with a commonality of destinies - explicable within their textual perspectives and literary lucidities,

A proximity of impulses, aspirations, experiences, characterized through the tight tailcoat of a courtier and minister, on the one hand, and a loose quilted chapan[2] on the other.

---

[1] Caucasian of Central Asian mountain village
[2] Central Asian quilted dressing gown

As such, these twinning consonances become overwhelming. Multi-faced, multilayered, fateful and Luciferian. The last term shedding light on "CONSONANCE" as a word used to name my research-essay on Goethe's "Night Song of the Wanderer": a concept represented (as it turned out), by the ancient Greek poet Alcman, while brilliantly arranged into the Russian and Kazakh languages by Lermontov and Abai, respectively.

Nonetheless, this essay is not about ideological; thematic, or for that matter artistic and aesthetic parallels hidden inside the "Night Song of the Wanderer".

Instead, my wish is to talk about Goethe and Abai from the standpoint of poetic spirits - of what Pushkin called the union of "magical sounds, feelings and thoughts".

Orchestrations differing in tone, no doubt, as well as in attitude and world perception, but always ultimately joined by the deepest sympathies.

So, I confess to being staggered by the fact our literary scholars were not interested in this topic previously.

* * *

Be that as it may, doesn't all this sound like subjectivism? Isn't it an outrageous claim, a mere whimsy? Surely, it simply "drags readers by the hair" - as the Germans say?

On reflection, possibly both of these observations may have a little truth – Goethe and Abai – being great poets, national geniuses, incarnations of their era and so on. But context isn't everything and occasionally more profound realities can be discerned beneath it. Indeed, in postmodern literature where miraculous displacements in time and space prove revealing, there is a diachrony, which uncovers asynchronized layers. For instance, in the famous novel by Anna Seghers "Meeting in the way" the authors Gogol, Hoffman and Kafka meet and have an animated conversation in a Prague café. All demonstrating that fictive devices free the imagination to describe a significance beyond simple history. Additionally, we need to recall the wisdom of our forebears when they stated a poet is a poet's kunak[3] - by which they

---

[3] Friend (among the mountain-dwellers of the Caucasus)

appear to have meant in mystical sympathy with each other. Thus, we stand firmly on the platform of intersubjective textual foundations by talking about the harmony of spirit: about a holistic perception of poetics and a correlation of the Muses (understood as sources of inspiration), along with solid letters and suggestive documents.

Lastly, I need to remind readers, that even hearing the name of Goethe arouses in our minds a rich, capricious, associative, array of signs and symbols mapping a specific time and place. A background whereon Engels says this "tremendously great" organic thinker held sway. However, as a man, this Olympian amid Europeans ironically intuited a crossroads in epochs. He felt "Storm and Stress" within himself, even though surrounded by a brilliant galaxy of German scientists, poets, and philosophers. Indeed, the Weimar Republic was the epicenter of civilization at that time, albeit one coming to an end.

Reminiscent of Friedrich Schiller's theatrical revolution. Each innovator begging the question who is Faust"? A titan in human form? A Regent of thought? The final conclusion of earthy knowledge - one who fights for life and freedom every day? Endless speculative editions and translations in most languages of the world are still debating these issues.

Abai's name equally arises at this juncture, even though outwardly looking much paler, almost faded. Akin to the patter of hoofs on the steppe, or the hollow murmur of a dombra[4]. By contrast, he is seen against a backdrop of interpatrimonial intrigues and fights. Fierce barymta[5] Folk songs, tales, dastans[6], kissas[7] - and an inexhaustible source of picturesque, eloquent-sounding words. Completely fatigued he once penned: "Here comes hoary age. Thoughts are sorrowful, sleep is light" and Inquiring despair, a heartfelt cry as well as "Where is he, a man, able to heed the word?" Sentiments from a small collection of poems (only 56!), published five years after the author's death...

Different epochs. Different historical and cultural environment. Different historical experiences. Different levels of civilization.

---

[4] Kazakh folk plucked two-stringed musical instrument with pear-shaped body and very long neck.
[5] Among the Turkic monadic peoples, capturing cattle as a way of revenge for the insult or compensation for damages.
[6] Epic in folklore and literature of the Middle East, Southest Asia.
[7] Sagas, historical poems.

Everything is different. Yet reflective? Goethe's contemporaries, after all, were Bukhar-zhyrau[8] Kalmakan-uly, the wise storyteller, who boldly taught the most formidable Khan Ablay, and Kuleke-uly, nicknamed Shalom-akyn[9]. Dulat, Shortanbay, and the rebellious warrior Mahambet Utemisov. Additionally, Goethe's "age mate" was Irgizbay, batyr[10], leader and influential biy[11].

Moreover, we must take into account the fact any research regarding Goethe and Abai has, until now, focused on dissimilarities. For Russians, and possibly all foreign readers, Abai could be a myth: a blank page. Inadequate translations giving rise to discrepancies in the Kazakh and Russian languages about him. So, for the time being Abai is a prisoner of his own national language. In this connection, I recall a sigh of despair in an article by professor Makhmudov H.H. ("Prostor", no.5, 1972): "Oh, if at least a few works of Abai were translated into Russian or English, French, German, Polish and other language, then Abai Kunanbayev would have taken his place on the podium of world poets!" I found a cutting of this article in the folders of my deceased friend Medeubay Kurmanov- Goethe connoisseur, and translator of "Faust" into the Kazakh tongue. This inscription - made by the hand of Medeubay on the sidelines of this quote - read: "Oh, if only!..." as a secret desire.

What is it all about? Where is that magical thread linking Goethe and Abai together? Where is the witching point of contact, which allows scholars to speak about the phenomenal commonality of these great personalities' way of thinking?

Steadfastly, I continue to claim it exists. This magical thread of spiritual closeness and togetherness of geniuses. It exists!

As the poet from the "Theatrical Introduction" to "Faust", says:

> *Often, when the first years are done, unseeing,*
> *It appears at last, complete, in deepest sense.*
> *What dazzles is a Momentary act:*
> *What's true is left for posterity, intact.*
>
> *(translation into Russian by Pasternak B.)*

---

[8] Representative of a certain genre of Kazakh historical poetry writing.

[9] Akyn – poet.

[10] Among Turkic peoples – dashing rider, man of courage, very strong man.

[11] Turkish title and rank, military and administrative, coming originally from the Common Turkic bək - chief.

And Abai constantly calls for "a thinking man, with fire in his chest" *(«көкірегінде оты бар ойлы адам»)*, to have thoughtful words, to evaluate the word *(«әр сөзін бір ойланып, салмақтасаң»)*, to a word that is kind, golden inside and silver outside *(«іші алтын, сырты күміс сөз жақсысы»)*, that warmly caresses one's heart *(«жүрекке жылы тиіп»)*.

Following the advice of Goethe and Abai, therefore - to grasp the deep meaning of their words, one discovers a soulful essence -"But Word, please, be unique, older than us you are, but always young" – says Goethe. Additionally, "Do not believe words for no reason, think over their essence and explore it" says Abai. So, deprived of studious glances, we can understand the truth, which proceeds across generations along a path of cognition. Through a thoughtful reading the great poets we are able to find philosophical and aesthetic similarities within their creative impulses and motives.

In this sense, the unembraceable (as I would like to call it), topic of Abai and Goethe interweaves at all times.

Marx in the preface to "The Capital", said: "Any nation can and should learn from others".

Undoubtedly accurate, this premise is true both to Goethe and Abai. Each of them eagerly and purposefully learned from others and constantly called their people to master the cultures of humankind, Yet, we cannot categorically state Abai learned from Goethe (or from German literature) specific subjects, or that his works had experienced the beneficial effects of the "greatest German" in specific parameters. There is no question of direct influence in this case. Nevertheless, one can hint about a philosophical and aesthetic harmony amongst these two spiritual giants.

Curiously, the relationship of culture and literature (in a broad philosophical sense) is extraordinary multi-faced. For instance, academician V.M.Zhirmunskiy found a familiarity of motifs in the Scottish ballad "Edward" and the Kazakh epos "Kozy Korpesh – Bayan Sulu"[12]. Isn't that interesting? Again, we may take the so-called motif

---

[12] Kazakh lyrico-epic poem of XIII-XIV centuries, written down in the middle of XIX century. Ancient legend of tragic love between Kozy Korpesh, young man, and Bayan Sulu, young lady, which were betrothed before they were born, but were parted by Bayan's father.

of invulnerability regarding Siegfried, Achilles, Isfandiar ("Shah-name" by Ferdowsi[13]), and Alpamis[14], which also drew the attention of V.M, Zhirmunskiy.

Or the famous specialist in Germanic Studies N.N. Vilmont who wrote the voluminous book "Dostoevsky and Schiller", wherein he uncovers a philosophical, aesthetic, ethical, psychological, artistic and literary affinity in the works of German romanticists and geniuses of Russian realistic literature. Furthermore, N.N. Vilmont even considers a parallel between Dostoevsky and Dante, since in "Crime and Punishment" a "Dante thematic" is caught up in the destruction and resurrection of a human personality.

Connectedly, I recall the very significant commentary notes of musicologist A.V. Zataevich to works of innumerable Kazakh folk singers-composers. In his unique collection "1000 songs of the Kazakh people" (1925) are often found such telling phrases as: "a lovely, almost Lohengrin-like melody", "the theme is in the temper of melodic patterns by Rubinstein" while it "reminds of the Bayan song in "Ruslan and Lyudmila" and "sounds like the song of Varangian's guest from the "Sadko" opera" as well as "Breton song" from the "Collection of French folk songs". Additionally, "the introduced song has something similar with Mussorgsky" and "the concluding part reminds us of the ending of Iontek from "Halka" by Moniuszko" along with "magnificent cantilena, doing credit to any of European composers" and so on. Needless to say, the Kazakh folk-composers, that are so emotively described by A.V. Zataevich had never heard of the musical works mentioned here. Yet, the spiritual echo (the consonance), is evident.

This is the perspective, the background, I consider necessary (and fruitful) to establish my "Goethe and Abai" theme.

It is known that Makhtay Auezov, the unsurpassed connoisseur of Abai,, had clearly and accurately identified the genesis of this great Kazakh poet: Kazakh oral folk arts, oriental poetry and Russian literature - and through it European literature. The last in the mentioned

---

[13] "The Book of Kings"- outstanding monument of Persian literature, national epic of the Iranian people.

[14] Folk heroic epic, existing as separate legends among a number of Turkic peoples. Central character is epical hero Alpamis, main cycle about his deeds, apparently, emerged in 14-17 centuries.

range of Abai's sources is still insufficiently (not to say poorly), studied by literary science. I am talking about Western European literature in relation to Abai's works.

In such a manner the association of "Goethe and Abai" powerfully suggests itself.

As such, I am convinced interesting observations and discoveries are awaiting any researcher. Starting, as this does, from comparisons of literary fact, to the identification of explicit and implicit analogues, ideas, creative insights and doubts. Thereafter continuing by the establishment and analysis of broader historical and cultural conclusions and generalizations, to the identification of specific patterns in large-scale volumes.

One more thing is notable: the association of Goethe with Abai is not dispassionate, not abstract and not academic - as it may seem at first glance. Rather, it vividly excites the modern reader. For example, I was delighted and, at the same time surprised, by readers responses to my articles "How does Faust sound in Kazakh?" (1983), "More attention to the valuable heritage" as well as "Goethe and Abai" (1985), published in "Kazakh adabiyoti".

Indeed, I received a lot of lengthy and interesting letters from my readers. I remember excited discussions, following my speech on this subject to the Evening University of Culture. A number of literary scholars adding their observations and concerns about this topic. One of them (Esen Geldy Zhakupov), even told me how, (consistently emphasizing the profound philosophy behind Abai's poetry), Mukhtar Auezov repeatedly said it is this quality of Abai's that makes him strikingly close to Goethe. This was the first time I had heard such comments and I was very happy: the observation was very insightful.

* * *

Of course, it is obvious, that Johann Wolfgang von Goethe could not have known Abai Kunanbayev ..... although what crosscurrents existed at that time only the angels can ever really understand.

Acknowledged so, Goethe himself tuned to the heat of pungent smells, keen sensuality, and the bright flowery picturesquenes of Oriental poetry. In other words, eastern genres replete with techniques mirroring his own interests. Thusly, his unique "West-Eastern Divan" (a poetic hymn to love and beauty) reveals a catechism to life-affirming spiritual humanism - which is Goethe's true credo. As such, he sings, "Who wants to know a poet, should go the poet's land". All sentiments affirming this fundamental thesis of unity beneath our world. As he eulogizes,

> *Gottes ist der Orient!*
> *Gotten ist der Okzident!*
> *God created the East,*
> *The West was his creation, too.*
>   *(Translation into Russian by Levik V.)*

However, had Abai heard of Goethe? If yes, to what extent? Can one ever hope to answer this question? Maybe , speculations will need to extend themselves by asking whether Abai, (in his "Gakliya"), or his contemporaries, ever mentioned the name of Goethe?

Weirdly, there are many reasons for asserting that Abai knew about Goethe – through numerous translations into Russian, quotations in countless magazine articles, the works of Russian critics, and from conversations with exiles - his disgraced friends.

Furthermore, it is well-known that Abai closely studied Pushkin, Turgenev, Gogol, Lermontov, Dostoevsky, Saltykov-Shchedrin, Tolstoy, Belinsky, Chernyshevsky, Dobrolyubov, Pisarev, Nekrasov. A highly persuasive fact, since within the critical works of these writers Goethe is irremovably present. Indeed, he is often quoted, referenced, debated, admired or subverted. Overall, it is not easy to count the times his name is mentioned in the works of those writers listed above.

So, Abai could not avoid Goethe's name. Especially because Abai also took an interest in Sociology, History, Culture, Enlightenment, and Economics. .

Undeniably, he read the works of philosophers like Plato, Spencer and Spinoza. This is reflected in his philosophical and ethical essays "Gakliya"[15]

---

[15] Words of Edification", "Book of words" – fundamental work of Abai, consisting of 45 short parables and philosophical treatises.

What is more, Abai's nephew, Kakitay Iskak-uly Kunanbayev (author of an obituary written in memory of the poet, published in "Semipalatinskiy listok" in 1905, and prefaced to the first collection of Abai's poems, also published by Kakitay in St. Petersburg in 1909), witnesses that Abai loved to read Lewis, Draper and other writers.

For his part, George Kennan - the American traveler and journalist recounts: Abai read the books of James Mill, Henry Thomas Buckle, George W. Draper and was "strongly interested" in English and West European philosophers. He then added, "We talked twice about Draper's book "From the history of social thought in Europe", wherein he showed a profound knowledge of the subject".

Interestingly, in his book "Siberia and exile" (1906), he warmly describes an evening with young exiles in Semipalatinsk - some of which were friends with Abai.

According to Kennan, during that evening numerous authors were mentioned and extracts read aloud from Shakespeare, Balfour, Stewart, Heine, Hegel, Lange, Irving, Cooper, Longfellow, Bret-Hart and Harriet Beecher Stowe[16]. It can be assumed, therefore, that Abai's range of reading was broad, diverse, and serious. Meanwhile, historians and literary scholars still need to pronounce on the memories of this poets contemporaries and descendants when they testify on the erudition of Abai, the steppe dweller. Hence, when Kakitay calls him a person of natural gifts, it is somewhat unsurprising. Particularly since his "Gakliya" names Homer, Socrates, Sophocles, Aristodim, Zeuxis, Joan of Arc ("Jane Arc"), Babur and many others, while among his translations into the Kazakh language one comes across Pushkin, Lermontov and Krylov, along with poems by Mickiewicz, Byron, I, Bunin. A. Delvig, Y. Polonsky, and Friedrich Schiller.

The elder brother of Abai (Russian officer Halilolla Uskenbaev), was also distinguished by his varied interests, erudition and education. Unarguably, G, N, Potanin reports in his memoirs "In the yurt[17] the last Kyrgyz prince": "told about one Kyrgyz sultan (the late Uskenbaev, who had finished his course for the Omsk Cadet Corps

---

[16] Refer to Myrzahmetov M., *Абай жүрген ізбенен*, Almaty, "Kazakhstan", 1985, page 148.

[17] A conical tent, traditionally made of animal skins upon wooden poles

- and then lived in his homeland in the steppe near Semipalatinsk - that he loved to tell his countrymen the content of Russian stories and novels. Furthermore, as the Kyrgyzs were listening to him, they asked him to write down these stories. Thus, a notebook containing free translation of the works of Turgenev, Lermontov, Tolstoy and others, was created. Sometimes, during these literary evenings in the yurt, Kyrgizs would start discussions and then, according to eyewitness, one could hear Uskenbayev use Russian authorities in debate: "Listen, this is what the well-known Russian critic Belinsky says about that", or "This is the opinion of Russian critic Dobrolyubov[18]".

Valuable evidence regarding the topic of our conversation.

I repeat here all of these well known facts with the sole purpose of convincing readers that someone as well read and inquisitive as Abai must have been aware of Goethe. To what extent – that is another question.

Looking back, thirty to forty years during the last century were the apogee of interest in Goethe for Russian journalism. Although Goethe remained thereafter a very popular personality within Russian literary circles. Indeed, Russian literary magazines of the 19th century were filled with translations of Goethe's materials. They were consistently and plentifully published in the "Contemporary", "Notes of the Fatherland", "Russian Thoughts", "Messenger of Europe" and "Bee" amongst other sources.

Meanwhile, a spiritual maturity regarding Abai falls in the eighties and nineties of the last century. After all, these year saw a particular fondness for translating Pushkin, Lermontov, Krylov as well as other autobiographical works.

With this in mind, the writings of Goethe, accompanied by numerous reviews on translations by Huber, Strugovshchikov, Vronchenko, Weinberg, Fet abounded. Moreover, this was the time when the collected works of Goethe were published. Even "The Conversations of Goethe" were collected by Eckermann" and published as separate editions in 1891, translated by D.P. Averkiev.

---

[18] "Russkoe bogatstvo" (Russian Wealth), 1986, no.8, p.83

Can one assume this huge stream of literature about Goethe had fully passed from the consciousness of thoughtful and curious readers of the City library of Semipalatinsk, named after Gogol, i.e. Abai Kunanbayev?

Hardly...

What is more, among friends of Abai were the "Russian" Germans – E,P, Michaelis and Bleck – men tightly bound to Abai through twenty years of sincere friendship. "Michaelis opened my eyes to the world" – confessed Abai. As for Alexander Lvovich Bleck, he was in exile at Semipalatinsk between 1883-1884. Once there, he worked for the Statistical Committee. A group later electing Abai to organize its museum and library. Thus, it is hard to assume that their meetings never mentioned the name of Goethe.

Here it is useful to recall that Bleck, (according to G. Kennan), spoke French and German, while he read English. Furthermore, he had a very carefully selected library, contacted "The Society of Translators and Publishers" in Moscow and, one believes, discussed innumerable topics pertinent to translators of Russian poetry into the Kazakh language.

Hence, one must assume that Abai - an admirer and translator of Pushkin - did know of the "Scene from Faust" within which the memorable dialogues of Mephistopheles and Faust take place. And that Abai knew Pushkin's famous words about the creation of "Faust" as the greatest embodiment of rebellion. At the end of the day, this work represents the spirit of modern poetry in a manner similar to the way the "Iliad" encapsulated classical antiquity.

Finally, Abai brilliantly translated "The Night Song of the Wanderer" through Lermontov's "Mountain Peaks" - «Қараңғы түнде тау қалғып...» Indeed, within the journal "Notes of the Fatherland" as in all the poetry collections of Lermontov this poem is called "From Goethe". Consequently, Abai must have known who authored the beautiful original.

Жүрегімнің түбіне терең бойла,
Мен бір жұмбақ адаммын, оны да ойла.
Соқтықпалы, соқпақсыз жерде өстім,
Мыңмен жалғыз алыстым, кінә қойма!

Abai

Genie fie mdfrig Fiill' und Segen,
Vernunft sei iiberall zugegen,
Wo leben sich des Lebens freut.
Dann ist Vergangenheit bestandig,
Das Ktinftige voraus lebendig,
Der Augenblick ist Ewigkeit.

Goethe

This much is measurable.

As for Goethe not being named in the verse and prose of Abai... well... one can never know who else remains unnamed. For instance, the quantrain «Кең жайлау — жалғыз бесік жас балаға» is actually a translation of "Child in the Cradle" by Friedrich Schiller, even though Abai doesn't mention Schiller's name either. Further: «Көңілім менің қараңғы, бол, бол, ақын!» goes back to Byron. Lermontov indicated the sources, although Abai doesn't name Byron. It is obvious "Of Experience" by Montaigne was equally familiar to Abai, but one will not come across the name of the French philosopher and essayist in his works.

Thus, it is the same with Goethe.

Generally, Abai seems reluctant to quote. Rethinking, as he does, a lot of things in his own way. Retelling ideas, as it were, in a very peculiar manner - poetically and aphoristically, in a "Kazakh" style. Hence, he uses a language comprehensible to his listeners. In other words, he would meditate on the thoughts of his time.

Fascinatingly he would take any maxim and transpose it so as to expand its boundaries. Thereby adapting it to the social background of the Steppe.

Sometimes, however he made clear links:

> For the edification of future generations
> Wiseman Dauani —
> Uttered so, the truth-teller.

Indeed, literary scholars have found that by the name of "Dauani" was meant Muhammad ibn Askhad (Zhalleddin) al-Dauani.

Yet, such references to a source in Abai's works are scarce.

Stated so, it is known Mukhtar Auezov thoroughly studied the so-called reading circle surrounding Abai and pointed to numerous original sources (which had taken endless exotic forms), through open retelling and mischievous quotation. Put differently, through the consonances and affinities reflected in Abai's poetry and philosophical prose. It is clear that some sayings, passing words and phrases, ethical and philosophical categories and definitions (such as *«якини иман»*— conscious faith and *«иман так лиди»* — blind faith remain exploratory, however.

This admitted, his experimental vocabulary examines three separate expressions for Self: moral personality, soul ("me") and flesh. Interesting contrasts between concreteness and abstractness also arise, along with three kinds of love. A "force of attraction of homogeneity", an "impressionability of the heart" and so on. Delineations discovered in art and scientific treatises which equally attracted his attention. All exemplified by notations on the medieval historians Ibn al-Athir, Rashid-ad-Din, Muhammad Gaidar, the collections of Akhmad Yassavi, Sufi[19] Allayar and Suleyman Bakyrgani, poetic creations by Hafiz, Nizami, Saadi, Rumi, Jami, and entries from endless encyclopedias as well as dictionaries. Tellingly, the four-volume epic "Abai's Path" references many famous authorities debated by Abey's reading circle. Explaining why, Mukhtar Auezov (an expert on the life and work of Abai) claims: "Having thrown a thin chapan over his shoulders and put on his light cap made of goatskin, Abai took his glasses and reached for a pile of books, lying beside his bed.

There, next to his everlasting companions - Pushkin and Lermontov, - now appeared Byron in Russian translation".

A remarkably, important detail.

No, I haven't a single doubt that Abai understood Goethe and his work. This essay is built on that belief.

* * *

There will probably be a lot of digressions and off-site comments with or without reason. So, I consider it necessary to say few words about the topic of productivity in art – Goethe talked about this often and willingly.

Another skeptic might say, "Goethe and Abai ... are they comparable? Are these personalities congenial? Are their creations analogous? Goethe's writings are difficult to embrace or perceive since they amount to more than ten volumes! How much was written by Abai? Poems,

---

[19] Professor of Sufism, or Tasawwuf – mystical-ascetic trend in Islam, one of the main trends of classical Islamic philosophy.

translations, philosophical and ethical studies, three dastans, research on the origin of the Kazakhs, together with comments— all of them barely making two volumes. What is there to compare?"

Yet, structuring the question this way is completely wrong. Firstly, I do not compare, or oppose, these giants. Their greatest peaks are distinctive and significant in themselves. Secondly, spiritual heritage cannot undergo quantitative evaluation. In his reflections on poetry and the importance of art, Abai repeatedly spoke about this matter.

Assuredly, reading Abai always seems to produce an extraordinary freedom of thought and a breadth of vision. One line of meditation being a honed philosophical formula giving cause to extended contemplation, while another induces a systematic worldview or outlook. Nonetheless, everything is a check and a balance in life. When envisioning Goethe one may imagine his formal, close-fitting frock covering an occasionally sloppy poet who engaged in frivolous antics, whereas Abai - in his baggy camel chapan - appears strikingly self-disciplined, neat, and aesthetically rigorous. Most of all he finds odious all sorts of truisms.

Thusly, we shall recount only one poem by Abai:

Тоты құс түсті көбелек
Жаз сайларда гүлемек.
Бәйшешек солмақ, күйремек,
Көбелек өлмек, сіремек.

Адамзатқа не керек:
Сүймек, сезбек, кейімек,
Қаракет қылмақ, жүгірмек,
Ақылмен ойлап сөйлемек.

Әркімді заман сүйремек,
Заманды қай жан билемек?
Заманға жаман күйлемек,
Замана оны илемек.

Moths whose outfit is bright,
Flowers say hello to you.

But the storm frightens you, and the garden is laid -
And they do not fly back.
All people are granted in a row,
A series of successes and losses,
That has always tantalized with doubts
And that is the answer they always want.
Time pursues all – young and old.
One would be happy to take off the burden of evil hinders!
Life is melancholy while laughter, shines and fumes,
Time comes, and you are taken by death.
(interlinear translation)

(Translation into Russian by Petrovs M.)

I found it necessary to introduce the original here in parallel with the translation since the translation (with its artistic merits and formal proximity) is still too concretized and – how should I say – devolved to a banal level. Primitivized, as it is, beneath general philosophical meaning. For example, the last stanza in a prose retelling suggests: "We all are puppets of an epoch; who is given the right to rule Time? Only nothingness reigns beyond time, yet who will trample upon it".

This result is quite different from the translation, isn't it? After all, "Life is melancholy while laughter, shines and fumes" is a flat truism, atypical of Abai.

Or let's consider the poem "When I die, will I become the earth?" Intriguingly, twenty-eight lines contain the whole of human life - its hardships, unequal struggles, dignity and tragic destiny. It is the confession of a "man with a mystery", as the poet calls himself. Even though it is a cordial, very honest, and sincere talk about himself and his future descendants, "Make compassion, my descendant, with one who was sorrowful and lonely", and "Struggled with the darkness as best he could... Don't take me amiss!", as well as "Judge, but remember guilt might be terrible, while there is no need to punish twice for one sin, and I paid in full for every single thing", - laments Abai. Any analysis of this poem - as solemn and majestic as Goethe's *Precept*, or Pushkin's *Monument* - would take another essay to uncover. Especially if one intended to examine the hidden axiology haunting every word.

Argued differently, his philosophical montage "Gakliya" makes an extremely short, concise treatise, which reflects on pressing moral, social and public issues. Indeed, vast thoughts are served up in a spoonful of words.

Such stylistics are characteristic of Abai. He knew the value of each and every word. Moreover he used them wisely. Critics commenting on his writing as concise, albeit delightfully flexible, in expression. As we may read,

'The most beautiful thought fades on passing through human lips", and

"A son that respects his father alone is an enemy of the people; a son of the people is also your friend", as well as

"Anger without power is a widower; a scientist without followers is a widower; love without faithfulness is a widow".

(Translation into Russian by Sanbayev S.)

The original being even shorter and dynamic.

That is why, I think, there are so many losses when translating Abai intro Russian: original lines just does not fit into this language. Furthermore, Abai's verse is multidimensional, with many interrelated meanings. As such, it sometimes doesn't suit interlinear translation in the least, unless one picks a dozen meanings and then writes a lengthy commentary on each choice.

A linguistic feature noted by the famous Kazakh prose writer Taken Alimkulov. A man who wrote a brilliant study on Abai with the evocative title "Man of Mystery". To my understanding, this is one of the most striking works in Abai Studies. So, speaking of Abai's poem "When I die, will I become the earth?", Alimkulov fascinatingly remarks: "I could have written a book on this poem. But I won't. Because the excess in analysis dilutes the theme. This is the first thing. And secondly, it is possible to write a book, or, if not, then at least a special article on each of Abai's poems". What is more, the researcher quoted Mukhtar Auezov as saying: "Abai is a deep river. I only drew upon it with a ladle"[20]

---

[20] *Т. Әлімқұлов, «Жұмбақ жан».* Almaty, "Zhazushy", 1978, p. 56.

These words – both of Auezov and Alimkulov – are hardly an exaggeration, nor enthusiastic hyperbole.

This is exactly what Goethe meant when he said to Eckermann: "And I should add that it is not the number of things created or accomplished that determines productivity in a man. We know poets who are considered to be very productive because their verses are being published volume after volume. But I would bluntly call them unproductive, for what they have made is deprived of life and strength"[21].

Here it is - the criterion of true talent: something that has life and strength.

Goethe also brought up the topic of "Strength" in coming generations" during his discourse on Hugo, "But if he hopes for a strong life in generations to come, he should think about how to write less and work harder".

All in all, the legacy of Abai, contained as it is within two small volumes, fully and adequately meets this criterion of productivity: a fact proved by the duration of his work.

The unsuspected side effect of this definition being its resonance with the concept of "genius". Indeed, Raphael, Mozart, Shakespeare, and ,obviously, Goethe, are clearly carriers of this "spiritual productivity". As the German scholar N. N. Vilmont says: "For Goethe, the problem of immortality is inextricably linked to the concept of productivity. Immortality is not given, but prescribed to the human: the more productive a human is, the more immortal he is".

The logic of these arguments applies to Abai – especially in terms of spiritual productivity, which is almost synonymous with immortality. Isn't this exactly what Abai meant by stating the following:

But is it possible to say one who gave the world immortal words is dead?

(Translation into Russian by Ozerov L.)

---

[21] Eckermann I.P. Conversations with Goethe. Moscow, Imaginative literature, 1981, p. 563.

The quantity of works, written about Goethe, is almost infinite. Even the effort to imagine this Mont Blanc of literature (on Goethe Studies) is frightening: one would lose ones nerve regarding it.

Additionally, a lot of scientific research has been written about Abai (literary works about him are around four thousand items) while it is impossible to number his indirect works. And yet, it seems to me that the true, hidden, and mysterious depth of Abai ("I am a man of mystery, think about that as well") has not been disclosed to date: nor has it been mastered or comprehended.

Maybe this is impossible?

After all, in order to comprehend Abai in all his spiritual power and diversity, it is necessary to climb to the same peak - not to look at his majestic figure from the height of insignificant bumps. But who is able to do that?

Abai is immeasurably deeper than we can comprehend at the moment. As a phenomenal individual, he is even deeper that his works. Although, this is not a paradox. The multifaceted work of Goethe is also not the whole Goethe himself.

A fact recognized by the sensitive and wise Jambul. In 1940, during celebrations of the 95th anniversary of the birth of Abai, the old akyn - having stared at his portrait - uttered:

Терең ойдың түбінде теңізі бар,
Тесіле көп қарасаң көңіл ұғар.
Сол тереңге сүйсініп жан үңілмей,
Есіл сабаз ызамен өткен шығар!

At the bottom of his deepest thoughts lies the sea,
That only the watchful eyes of a soul can comprehend.
No one, it seems,
Had looked into that depth with love,
And this great good man passed away with grief and anger.

(interlinear translation)

What an exact, soulful perseption! What a convincing testimonial!

This poem is called "To the portrait of Abai". A work wherein we may read such words as:

Ақыл, қайрат, білімді тең ұстаған
Өр Абайдың төтеген кім бетіне?

> *Endowed with knowledge, energy*
> *And mind in equal measure,*
> *Who dared to contradict proud Abai?*
>
> *(interlinear translation)*

All making me immediately recall the poem by V. A. Zhukovsky "To the portrait of Goethe":

> *Having accepted bold freedom as his law,*
> *He floated over the world as omniscient thought. And he beheld*
>   *every little thing around—*
> *And did not resign himself to anything.*

Again, almost the same sentiments (let alone words) are used by poet Boratynsky in his poetic response to the death of Goethe:

> *Being a winged thought,*
> *He floated around the world,*
> *Only in the infinite*
> *He has found his limit.*

Isn't it curious that in Zhukovsky's, appeal to the portrait of Goethe, and Jambul's eulogy to the portrait of Abai, each saw almost the same, or – at least – similar phenomena? Indeed, it is difficult to ignore the parallel in such lines as: "He beheld every little thing around" and "Endowed with knowledge, energy and mind in equal measure"; He floated over the world as omniscient thought". Or, according to Boratynsky, "Being a winged thought, He floated around the world" and "at the bottom of his deepest thoughts lies the sea". On top of which, the poet "did not resign himself to anything" while "who dared to contradict proud Abai?"

Such comparisons seem remarkable to me.

Doesn't it show us the magical relationship of multilingual poetic spirits?

All this, I think, is obviously contained inside Goethe's theory of spiritual productivity as genius. A spiritual productivity equally gifted to that great inhabitant of steppe Abai.

* * *

At this juncture, we need to pay attention to the genesis of Goethe and Abai. Here we shall also find many similarities and consonances.

Geniuses do not accidentally come into this world. Nature itself takes care of the progress of these human spirits. After all, society needs titans, and gives rise to titans. Belinsky notices in "The Works of Alexander Pushkin" that: "Nature creates the human, but society is the one that develops and forms him".

Goethe was born in 1749 in a remote, underdeveloped, region, which was tired of endless wars and princely feuds. Indeed, we know the sharp, deadly response Engels gave to the feudal Germany of that time. I will give just one sentence: "… disgusting rotting and a decaying mass".

Young Goethe, therefore, experienced acute dissatisfaction with squalid German reality; he bitterly hated German philistinism, expressed protested against the social order of his period with its "Storm and Stress" and constantly refers to legends that despise conventions within his rotten society; pettiness always depressed him.

This explains his departure for Italy. Certainly, his passion for the Greek myths, history, art, classicism and Latin poetry is the stuff of lore Furthermore, his self-confessed feeling of suffocation in a Germany, fragmented into hundreds of principalities and diminutive States drove him to despair. Hence, Goether looked for union with nature: a submersion into «Innerlichkeit»— a special type of contemplation, in order to escape from the harsh realities surrounding his own soul.

A futile search, perhaps.

For his part, Abai was born almost a hundred years later in the patriarchal-feudal steppe. An age-old location suffering from backwardness, spiritual isolation, and colonialism. All motives for mourning – "zarzaman"[22]. Nonetheless, Muslim bookishness and

---

[22] "Times of atonement" – poetic trend, expressing protest against the colonial policy of czarism, sorrow and mourning for the irretrievably departed times,

glimpses of Russian democratic culture alleviated the gloom. As did the rich nomads' camps he encountered while wandering across these majestic landscapes. Yet, vague anxieties affected him as a youth. Yet, where can he run? To the religious school in Semipalatinsk? How can he soothe his emotional turmoil?

Физули, Шамси, Сайхали,
Навои, Саади, Фирдоуси,
Хожа Хафиз — бу әмәси
Мәдет бер я шағири фәрияд.

Fizuli, Shamsi, Sayhali,
Navoi, Saadi, Ferdowsi,
Hodja Hafiz – all of you
Help my aspiration.

(interlinear translation)

All anxieties needing a resolution. But neither young Goethe, nor youthful Abai, had any idea about their future mission.

As we may read, "The father of Goethe was an imperial adviser to the city of Frankfurt and belonged to the local bourgeoisie. He was a calm, methodical, sensible, reasonable, prudent person, while at the same time a real burgher-formalist, representative of the type that was quite common in Germany" – according to A. Shakhov in *Goethe and his time*[23].

When reading such reports about Goethe's father carefully, one immediately recalls steppe Sultan Kunanbay the, father of Abai – as described in Zhidebay's tract.

Indeed, lets remember his colorful personality as a powerful feudal lord, as outlined by Auezov in his brilliant epic regarding this capricious, fierce, ruler.

A psychology mirrored by Goethe's father - who was known to be demanding and strict with his children. He was also renowned for

---

moral judgment over modernity.
[23] St. Petersburg, edition III, 1908. p. 33.

his perseverance, diverse skills and knowledge, furious ambition and determination. As such, it is difficult to call him ordinary person.

Again, dispositions reflected in Kinanbay, as Adolf Yanushkevich tells us after seeing Kunanbay in 1846:

"Kunanbay – well – he is some kind of machine like a clock that only stops working when it is unwound. Once he is awake, he sets his tongue in motion and speaks tirelessly until he falls asleep. Every minute Kirghiz people come to him - he is seen as an oracle, prophesying from his tripod - often supporting the sides with his arms; he quotes shariah[24] after every three words of his speech, and his memory is so wonderful, that he cites all the decrees and orders of the government as if he is reading them from a book"[25].

Now let's examine matrilineal lines of descent. Goethe's mother, Katharina Elizabeth Textor, according to contemporaries, was notable for her intelligence, kindness and cheerfulness. Indeed, Goethe, her elder son, believed he inherited from his mother poetic imagination. There is even a poem "To my mother" by Goethe, imbued with this deep sense of reverence, touching love, and gratitude.

As for Abai's mother, Ulzhan, she was a dignified, wise and respected woman. Even Kunanbay, a feudal lord to the bone, considered her his strength. Stated so, one of the best scenes of the epic "Abai's Path" is a dialogue between Ulzhan and Kunanbay when he betakes himself to hajj: the pilgrimage to Mecca. What dignity and composure! What generosity! Ulzhan equally endows her son Ibrahim (whom she tenderly calls Abai), with her sensitivities.

In himself, Abai never complained of childhood. "Six of us from father and four from mother - there was no reason to be lonely", he says in the "Octastich".

Thankfully, Goethe never knew hardship, never felt hunger nor fear. On the contrary, he lived in comfort: one might even say in luxury. Even though, he never thought of these conditions as an end in

---

[24] The Islamic legal system, derived from the religious precepts of Islam, particularly the Quran and the Hadith.

[25] Yanushkevich A., Diaries and letters from the trip to the Kazakh steppe, Kazakhstan, 1966, p. 184.

themselves. Rather, he regarded them quite calmly, resignedly or even indifferently.

Similarly, Abai never knew real hardship. Living, as he did, in prosperity and quite securely - in the traditional manner of unpretentious steppe peoples. Those who owned herds and flocks, while dwelling within rich white yurts. When regarding the hopeless indigence of his powerless fellow tribesmen, he simply expressed his understanding, compassion and empathy.

Other parallels follow. In his dreams as imperial advisor to the city of Frankfurt, Goether's father foresaw his son as a man developing a professional career. Certainly, at his urgent request in the spring of 1772 Goethe went to Wetzlar to review legal practices at the Imperial Court of Justice.

In this way, father wanted son to acclimatize to the Department of Justice. No doubt, there were disagreements between them, but it is recorded how Goethe regretted not managing "To establish good relations with my father...", - as one discovers in *From my life. Poetry and Truth.*

As if in echo, steppe Sultan Kunanbay pre-prepared a destiny for his son - which had nothing to do with poetry. Instead, he saw him as his worthy successor and associate. A manager for the hoi polloi; someone moderately educated, knowing laws, experienced in patrimonial disputes and the intrigues of the silver-tongued biy. To this end, he sent his son of ten years to Semey, a distant steppe town where he could attend a Muslim religious school.

As these celestial twins progressed, young Goethe came to feel no sympathy for his classes at the Imperial Court of Justice. Rather, he intensively studied the poets. "Mentally I set aside lessons in jurisprudence and devoted myself to languages, antiqueness, history and everything that followed from it. To be true to poetic expression I noticed in myself, in others, and in nature, has always given me the greatest joy", - recalled Goethe.

Concomitantly, Abai was not attracted by the study of religious scholasticism. It is known he secretly visited a Russian parish school without informing the mullahs[26], wherein he mastered Russian grammar. It was here that a thirst for knowledge and poetry arose in him.

Unsurprisingly, Goethe didn't stay in Wetzlar for long, while Abai studied in Semipalatinsk for only three years.

Looking back, the soul of Goethe was struck by poetic inspiration at a very tender age. His whole life being filled by a superhuman effort to work ever harder. A curiosity, since he was considered a spoiled child: the darling of fortune.

As for the other Gemini twin, no one could accuse this powerful lord's son of immaturity; he had not been a Frondeur murza[27], a steppe dandy, traveling around auls in search of pleasures. Rather, a maturity of soul came early to him. Family honour imposing huge civil responsibilities. Indeed, this young man's vulnerable heart disturbed his way of thinking. At least according to his nephew Kakitay.

It is said when he was fifteen years old, Abai would baldly interfere with patrimonial litigations, argued by highly experienced biys as an equal and that he mastered the skills of sheshen,[28] Moreover, he carried great weight among the common people as well as those who ruled them. Perhaps he felt well-being and satiety were only for philistines? Either way, when he was forty years old Abai complained of loneliness, fatigue, a lack of friends, mental confusion and pain. Despite being considered a bai[29] - an owner of herds promising delivery from grief.

Yet, these two soulmates never stopped being in an astral reciprocity, As such, Goethe once confessed to Ekkerman, "I have always been called the darling of fortune – I am not going to grumble about my fate or complain about life. But, in fact, all my life has been effort and hard work, and I can boldly say that for over seventy-five years I did not take a month free to have a good time. Instead, I had been tossing the stone, which did not lie down on its place in the end".

So much for this lucky man - the favorite of fortune!

---

[26] The word, used to refer to a Muslim man or woman, educated in Islamic theology and sacred law.

[27] A Princely title in Tatar states, such as Khanate of Kazan, Khanate of Astrakhan and others, and in Russia.

[28] Orator

[29] Rich landowner in Central Asia.

The same grim idea is expressed in Goethe's poem *Elegy* (1823):

> *Who the immortals' favorite erst was thought;*
> *They, tempting, sent Pandoras to my cost,*
> *So rich in wealth, with danger far more fraught;*
> *(translation into Russian by Levik V.)*

And how many bitter confessions Abai makes!

> *My satisfaction – nothing but illusion it is.*

Or:

> *"…Woeful thoughts, broken sleep,*
> *The spirit is inflamed with the poison of a sullen anger.*
> *No one to share my thoughts!"*

Or:

> *Exhausted, deceived be everyone around.*
> *I was betrayed both by foe and confidant.*

Or:

> *There is no life in my chest …*

Or:

> *My life is short,*
> *The goal is far,*
> *And there is scarcely strength in me.*

Or:

> *Thy family is grand,*
> *But there is no one to understand me,*
> *And I am alone among the people.*

Or:

My heart wears forty patches on it.

Or:

I fought alone against thousands…

And so on and so forth…
So much for the carefree, serene bai!
Relatedly, Goethe's confession about the stone " which did not lie down on its place in the end" is also remarkable. Doesn't it remind one of the cliff from which Abai cried vainly every day?

> *The same old cliff whined beneath me —*
> *The response is there, but it is empty.*

Isn't it this the same condition that Goethe and Abai speak about?
Goethe, "the Olympian", admits his whole life is "effort and hard work". Let us pay attention, therefore, to the verbs in the "Gakliya" which Abai uses to describe his life-journey. In the very first sentence of the *First word* we read: "struggled, knocked down, argued, competed – experienced evil to the heart's content"; in the next sentence: "my soul is tired, I am exhausted". After a few paragraphs, one learns: "There is no peace either in thy life, or in thy soul", whilst in the "Third Word""quarreled", "divided into parties", and "fought for power" are again employed. Equally, tragic questions are asked.
Questions perennially "accursed" since they inquire: how can one live? How may we be? What are we to do? I've counted: in the "First Word" eleven interrogative sentences, whereas in the "Tenth Word" – twenty eight, in the "Twenty-Third" – twenty four, in the "Fortieth Word" – forty four and so on. Truly, Abai is tormented by his doubts and questions constantly. Thenceforth, troubles disturb his soul, along with the souls of others - as if fulfilling the order of God to Mephistopheles in "Faust":

> *Mans energies all too soon seek the level,*
> *He quickly desires unbroken slumber,*
> *So I gave him you to join the number,*
> *To move, and work, and play the devil.*

(translation into Russian by Pasternak B.)

At first, Goethe writes clearly imitative poems - in accord with literary fashion: in a Rococo style. However, he didn't publish them, nor advertise these works. Instead, they remained in the albums of friends as part of a handwritten collection. Indeed, he gathered them later, when more self-confident. As Goethe recalls in *Poetry and Truth*: "... Long time no proven need for versification revived in me. I write a lot of songs for Frederica on familiar motifs. They would make a bulky volume; but only a few of them were preserved, and it is easy to find them among my other poems".

In similar vein, the early poems of Abai that have reached us are also imitative, with a clear touch of Muslim literacy, thickly interspersed with Arabic constructions, as well as the constructions of Farsi and Chagatai. Curiously, he attributed them to others, concealing his authorship until the age of forty, when he felt a poetic maturity and civil stability.

Eventually, of course, youth disappears. In the cases of Goethe and Abai, however, this signaled a period of persistent investigation into harmonic integrity through art, through the Word, and, obviously, through Poetry. Thusly, they could soothe and comfort mental confusion, overcome the misery of reality through aesthetic education, while surrounded themselves with the power and magic of high-brow, spiritualized expression.

"All of my poems – poems 'in the event of', they are inspired by the life, and they arise from it. And I snap my fingers at my 'off the mark' poems", - says Goethe.

In addition, Abai speaks about vital foundations in his poetry:

> *Poetry is master of the language,*
> *Genius carves the miracle from stone.*
> *(interlinear translation)*
> *(translation into Russian by Zvyagintseva V.)*

Or:

I make the verses not for fun.

I do not fill verses with fiction.
(interlinear translation)
(Translation into Russian by Brodsky D.)

Something almost identical is encountered in Goethe's works: "I do not write in order to please you, you should learn something!"

But neither Goethe, nor Abai can find the desired harmonic integrity in the environments they inhabited. In a sense, they were overtaken by disappointments far too often.

Getting off the path, I was friend to the crowds,
Having known you, I stand alone! -

Says Goethe sadly in his "Initiation", written in 1784.

One hundred years later, Abai echoed:

At the shaman's grave, I
Stand alone – the whole truth is mine!
(Translation into Russian by Ozerov L.)

"And finally, what is life for a German scientist? If there could be something good for me, then it was not customary to talk about it, while what was allowed discussion, wasn't worth it. And where are they, those listeners, to whom I would like to speak?" – asks Goethe sadly. The same idea is expressed in his poem "Disclosure of the Secret":

But where is the guardian of the word
that grasped the value of the Word?

Isn't this the same intonation that can be heard in the "First Word" by Abai? "And tormented by the thought - to what should I devote the rest of my days? What to do?" Further, isn't it is the same rhetorical question (in nearly the same language) that Goethe asked when Abai inquires, "Will there be a man who would heed my words?" Anyway, these uncanny resemblances continue. For example, in an effort to streamline and harmonize his surrounding, while hoping to improve the social order (yet, having lost his faith in the Stuermer rebellion, in 1775), Goethe becomes a courtier - a Minister of the small Saxe-

Weimar duchy of Karl August. As such, he leads the government of this diminutive State and gets involved with the mining industry, the construction of a theater and the natural sciences. He even seems to believe in enlightened absolutism at this stage. Nevertheless, during the ten years Goethe spent as a Minister at the Weimar court, his dreams slowly diminished and sobriety shaped his hopes.

Exactly one hundred years later, in 1875, Abai - hoping to educate people and improve their life - sought election to the position of parish governor in Konyr-Kokshe-Tobyktin. In this respect, he stood up for justice in the system, while taking care that public order became his responsibility. However, he was only in charge for three years, since this role clashed with his vocation as a poet. They were "two incompatible things", like genius and villainy.

Overtly reminiscent of Goethe when he undertook reforms at the Weimar palace Clearly, Goethe became interested in criminal law as he fought against corrupt brokers and land sub-purchasers, by trying to introduce new taxes that would make life for farmers easier.

Curiously, it is also known that Abai improved the legal code existing in the steppe at the time. Indeed, in 1885, he participated in the work of an extraordinary congress at Kara-Mole among clan representatives of the Middle Zhuz[30]. Certainly, they added very substantial "baps" (i.e., paragraphs, articles) to the draft of a new provision ("Erezhe"), exempting widows from cruel and degrading customs "amengerstvo"[31] - by enshrining their right of free choice in a spouse, while introducing humane legislation in the matter of punishment for theft and cattle lifting.

Yet, hopes can crumble and break like waves upon a shore. Often, forcing a person to similar conclusion to Werther in his farewell letter: «Alles in der Welt lauft doch auf eine Lumperei hinaus», when it says

---

[30] A zhuz (also translated as "horde" or "hundred") is one of the three main territorial and tribal divisions in the Kypchak Plain area that covers much of contemporary Kazakhstan, and represents the main tribal division within the ethnic grouping of the Kazakhs. The Middle zhuz or Argyn horde consists of six tribes, covering central and eastern Kazakhstan

[31] A type of marriage in which the brother of a deceased man is obliged to marry his brother's widow, and the widow is obliged to marry her deceased husband's brother, also known as levirate marriage.

"everything in this world ends up with nonsense". The very thing that is expressed in the Kazakh aphorism: *«Аяғы дүниенің ырым-жырым»*, "the end of life is the same as a tattered rag". The German «Lumperei» strikingly consonant with the Kazakh *«ырым- жырым»*.

Assuredly, Werther in Goethe's novel shares Abai's sentiment that:

> *Behind me is not life, but a dream that did not come true.*
> *I wish I had lived estranged from that bright dream.*

Or:

I

> *Өмірдің алды ыстық, арты суық,*
> *Алды — ойын, арт жағы мұңға жуық.*
> *The beginning of life is hot, the ending – ice cold.*
> *The game in the beginning and at the end is closer to sorrow.*
> > *(interlinear translation)*

Collective optimism does not satisfy Abai. For him. Fidelity to such ideals contradicts reality. Thus, the discord and disappointment in some of his poems.

Relief was discovered, however, by spiritual unity among people.

A fact both Goethe and Abai advocated within their works.

Goethe, for his part, always acknowledging himself to be a national poet. Albeit of a united Germany. And as such, he personified the best type of German commonality.

It is these circumstances to which SED paid attention in its manifesto on the 200th anniversary of Goethe in the newspaper "Neues Deutschland" (dated March 23, 1949), As such, we may read. "In fragmented and torn pieces of Germany, Goethe embodied the unity of the Germans in the sphere of spiritual life and language... To a large extent it is due to Goethe that German literature was exalted to the level of developed national literatures and found its way into the treasury of world culture.

It is also appropriate to recall that Goethe was the first to put forward the concept of "world literature".

Interestingly, Abai never limited himself to specific clan concerns. Consistently recognized himself as the national poet. Moreover, he passionately called the Kazakhs to unity: bitterly ridiculing and denouncing its opponents. Refusing, as he did, to only speak on behalf of "his" Tobykta kinsfolk.

As a man, he turned to the future. Always seeing the whole Kazakh people together. He even said: "Oh, my Kazakhs…" and "My native people!" Having admitted: "I gave my love to the people…" he also lamented:

> *He inspired, instructed:*
> *If Kazakhs aren't by friendship be bound,*
> *Then life will be hateful all around.*
> (Translation into Russian by Ozerov L.)

All deeply educated perspectives noted by the critic L.M Lenonov when he commented on Abai's personality by saying: "One really needs to have a winged mind and vision like an eagle to find a way towards the crossroad of historical destinies. One must have a powerful voice to tell people about things that can be seen from a subcelestial height, and finally, one needs to have rare courage to lift up ones voice in the conditions prevailing here a century ago… Such was Abai Kunanbayev – the beacon of his people"[32].

Evidenced, as these shared views are, by both Goethe and Abai in their work as truly national poets who rose to the peak of universal consciousness: an achievement linking them together.

In talking about the genesis of Goethe and Abai, it is easy to identify uncanny similarities and obvious parallels of their external biographies. More precisely, through the common motifs of their creative destiny. Furthermore, these couplings can go on and on. For example, we can recall all the beloveds of Goethe. Those by whom he became inflamed with passion at different times. All being endlessly described - as well as invariably enumerated - within literary references. Women such as Kathy Shënkopf, Friederike Brion, Lily Shëneman, Charlotte von Stein, Christiane Vulpius, Minna Hertslib, Marianne von Willemer and Ulrika von Lewetzov.

In addition, let us recall Dilda, Togzhan, Saltanat, Aygerim, Erkezhan as loves of Abai.

---

[32] Russians about Kazakh literature. Almaty, 1957, p. 87-88.

In Goethe's hedonistic case, tragedy overshadowed this part of his life. Many of his relationships becoming a spiritual crisis leading to a radical change in consciousness and a fascination with mysticism. As such, this Pandora's box – inevitably coloured his poetry: being mentioned inside text as telling witticisms. "Who searches is forced to wander", - as it says in "Faust".

By 1830 in Italy, Goethe's only son - August – had died. At which point, only his titanic workload saved him from spiritual collapse. Thusly, he wrote to his friend, the composer Zelter: "The most surprising and significant thing in this trial is that I ought to drag the burden all alone - and with even greater difficulty. Only the enormous concept of bonds can make us withstand these obstacles. I try to keep physical balance, the rest forms by itself. The body needs, the spirit wants – it means that a person who knows that his wishes are foreordained inevitably does not have to think twice... So, forward we go, through the graves..."

As a spiritual twin, Abai had also fully experienced grief, crises, shocks, the loss of loved ones, deaths of beloved sons, despair and sorrow. In sad moments, he turned to God in prayer, saying, "My heart bears forty patches" as well as lamentations such as. "My way was hard and thorny". Clearly, the death of his beloved son Abdurakhman almost crushed Abai.

As a pupil at Mikhailovsky Atrillery school in St. Petersburg and a lieutenant of artillery in Verniy, he died in 1895 at the age of twenty-seven years. All Abai could do in response was dedicate several poems to his memory. In one of them Abai speaks about him as follows:

He was the herald of the new day
I am rounding out the last century...
My grievous loss is hard!
It hurts!.. I am the old man...

I am broken into half by the grieve.
Bitter tears pour as a creek,
Like someone having lashed my eyes
With a whip with all his might.

(interlinear translation)
(Translation into Russian by Neyman U.)

There is a special language in sorrow. One that Abai shared with Goethe. A linguistic sensitivity translating into a knack for speaking many tongues. Indeed, Goethe knew a number of languages and even stated, "Who does not know other languages, knows nothing about his own". Hence, he read some of the great poets in the original. For his part, Abai, knew Russian, Arabic, Persian and Turkish languages. Allowing him to read Pushkin, Lermontov, Shchedrin, Omar Khayyam, Hafiz and Rudaki.

Extending his skills, Goethe painted, while Abai composed music to accompany his poetry.

Etc.

Maybe all this is coincidental? Mere facets of their personal lives? Perhaps so, but not regarding their historical missions, their destinies - or – to be more prosaic – the circumstances of spiritual necessity, which gave rise to Goethe and Abai as artists.

It is in these seemingly unconscious coincidences of fate that each titan became undoubted etheric kin.

Accordingly, Tomas Mann mused: "Any creative forces should serve the higher purpose of humanism - searching for true humaneness – is a life worthy of a Human".

So, Goethe and Abai are majestically consonant in their mutual devotion to this purpose.

* * *

One last deviation needs to be explored - the issue of metric prosody in poetry by Goethe and Abai.

To begin, one must remember that both the German and Kazakh languages are multi-structural, while tonic and syllabic versification are two very different things.

Possibly, the enormous service of Johann Wolfgang von Goethe lies in the formation and development of a normalized German language. After all, according to experts in German Studies, the process of combining national literature with inherited language (at the beginning of the 18th century) had not been completed. It required huge efforts, intense researches, violent disputes and the fruitful creative activity of German linguists, philosophers and writers. Certainly, all the fragmented German principalities needed to overcome dialectal features, local expressions, and provincial rules of pronunciation. In this, Goethe played an outstanding role through his multifaceted work. Even though, he, himself, had retained the characteristic features of Frankfurt speech, (as had Friedrich Schiller), tinged, as it was, with a Swabian lilt. So, we may read,

"Goethe used all the richness of rhyming possible in German, tried all the poetic dimensions, and diversified strophic construction of the poems. All that poetry in German was capable of - was implemented by Goethe", - says the researcher A.A. Anikst.[33]

The same can equally be said about Abai with regard to Kazakh poetry.

He is the founder of a new Kazakh literature and the creator of a literary language. Additionally, he consciously and persistently strived to expand semantic and rhythmic-melodic possibilities in Kazakh poetry: diversifying stanzas, verse lines and rhyme. Moreover, one may even speak about the introduction of syllabic elements in versification and toning via Abai. By himself, he introduced around two dozen new forms in Kazakh versification.

Again, reminiscent of Goethe expanding forms in German poetry. His "Roman Elegies", as a case in point, revived ancient metric systems, while, his "West-Eastern Divan" stretched received metric prosody due to its application of oriental contrivance.

Of course, this topic is huge. Still, in order to illustrate further obvious similarities in the reforming activities of Goethe and Abai, specific examples will help. Firstly, I would like to remind Russian readers that the most common form of Kazakh poetry is hendecasyllabic - traditional verse with AABA rhyming schemes. Another fundamental form is hepta-octosyllabic verse with interlaced rhymes adopting ABAB patterns. These styles are rooted in folk (poetic) inheritances, although they may be partially found in modern Kazakh poetry - especially Kazakh (syllabic) versification.

---

[33] Johann Wolfgang Goethe. Gedichte. Moskau. Progreb. 1980. S. 6

Interestingly, hendecasyllabic and hepta-octosyllabic verse with ABAB and AABA rhymes are often found in the poetry of Abai. In this respect, one only needs to look into his books.

For a Kazakh reader, I can say AABA rhyme is not peculiar to German versification (with the exception of translated or stylized poetry - it is not encountered in Goethe's works), although "knittelferz" (raeshny verse) can often produce couplets with the plain rhyme AABBCC and so on. A poetic form almost impossible in Kazakh poetry and merely suggested by the poetry of Abai.

Stanzas with an ABCB rhyme are equally infrequent visitors to Kazakh poetry, although one can encounter them in Abai's works. Contrarily one finds an abundance of them in works by Goethe. At this point, I will abstain from giving further examples – they are obvious.

Fascinatingly, Abai introduced sexysillabic verse into Kazakh poetry with cross-rhyme. Here an example would be appropriate:

> Қызарып, сұрланып,
> Лүпілден жүрегі,
> Өзгеден ұрланып
> Өзді-өзі керегі.
> To blush and to pale,
> With beating heart,
> Not to look at the others,
> To sigh about one another.

(interlinear translation)
(Translation into Russian by Tarlovsky M.)

Or:

> Ысытқан, суытқан
> Бойыңды бір көңіл.
> Дүниені ұмытқан
> Құмарың тозар, біл.
> Cold, heat ... young, old
> Everyone knew the power of passion
> But ,the spring of wondrous charms,
> The passion will disappear without a trace.

(interlinear translation)
(Translation into Russian by Petrovy M.)

Similar meter was not a stranger to Goethe either.

Tage der Wonne Kommt ihr so bald '
Schenkt mir die Sonne HUgel und Wald?

(*Fгйhzeitiger Fruhling»)

With their search for new forms of poetry both Goethe and Abai pursued the enrichment of musicality. of the poem as well.

As such, Goethe wrote a number of poems in folk-poetic spirit that begged for musical accompaniment. It was no accident, therefore, that they immediately attracted the attention of composers - and have now become well-loved songs in German-speaking countries. It suffices to recall the fate of the "Little wild Rose" *(«Heidenroslein»)*, in this regard, due to its narrative style, its melodiousness, and its light sadness.

Unarguably, musicality is in the very nature of his "Octastich" and "Hexastich". It is also no coincidence that Abai himself composed music for many of his poems. As academician Ahmet Zhubanov notes, "… Abai's songs were written not by an illustrator, but by a composer. They feature musical qualities and played a major role in the development of musical culture amongst Kazakh people".

Indeed, the "Ostastich" form is a genuine innovation of Abai;s.

Алыстан сермеп,
Жүректен тербеп,
Шымырлап бойға жайылған,
Қиуадан шауып,
Қисынын тауып,
Тағыны жетіп қайырған.
Толғауы тоқсан қызыл тіл,
Сөйлеймін десең өзің біл.

Calls from a distance,
Comes from the heart,
Makes us tremble;

> *It is sharper than anything,*
> *It is faster than anything,*
> *It can chain a doe.*
> *Many-sided, flexible language*
> *You are great in the mouth of a nation!*
> *(interlinear translation)*
>   *(Translation into Russian by Ozerov L.)*

The point here is not about the adequacy of the translation, but only about form - about the size of a poem. This can equally be said about external, formal, attributes.

Another curious fact is that Goethe also composed a kind of "octastich", although structurally it differs markedly from Abai's *"Сегіз аяқ"*. I am talking about Goethe's poem "To the New Year" («Zum neuen Jahr»), wherein each stanza consists of eight rhyming verses. Here, I will give just one stanza of the original:

> *Zwischen dem Allen,*
> *Zwischen dem Neuen,*
> *Hier uns zu freuen,*
> *Schenkt uns das Gluck,*
> *Und das Vergangne HeifSt mil Vertrauen Vorwarts zu schauen,*
> *Schauen zaruck.*

I suggest that any reader who does not know the original languages take a close look at the form of "octastich" used by Goethe and Abai. It is easy to see the two first verses of Abai are "pentasyllabics", while the third verse is "octosyllabic". Then comes symmetrical repetition, whereas the end stanza is completed by two octosyllabic verses with plain rhyme. The metre of Goethe's "octastich" is clearly organized traditionally albeit whimsically.

Contrastingly, the rhyming scheme of "octastich" as used by Abai is AABCCBDD, while the rhyming scheme of "octastich" by Goethe is ABBCDEEC.

Another innovation of Abai in Kazakh versification is *"алты аяк"* – "hexastich".

One example:
Бай сейілді,

Бір бейілді,
Елде жақсы қалмады.
Елдегі еркек
Босқа селтек
Қағып елін қармады.

The size and pattern of this stanza – even the sounds – immediately conjure associations with themes from the scene "Witch's Kitchen" in the "Faust" tragedy:

> *The light of cognition*
> *Is secret for everyone,*
> *For all of us, without the exception!*
> *Sometimes it is*
> *Like a gift, destined,*
> *Even to those who have no thinking.*
>   *(translation into Russian by Holodkovsky N.)*

Or let us recall Gretchen's song from "Faust":
> *Wohin ich immer gehe,*
> *Wie weh, wie weh, wie wehe Wird mir im Busen hier!*
> *Ich bin, ach! kaum alleine,*
> *Ich wein, ich wein, ich weine,*
> *Das Herz zerbricht in mir.*

> *Who then can feel,*
> *How like steel,*
> *Is the pain inside my bones?*
> *What my poor heart fears for,*
>   *(translation into Russian by Pasternak B.)*

We can bring in parallel "hexastich" stanzas from Abai's *"Бойы бұлғаң"* and Goethe's "Between the two worlds" *("Zwischen beiden Welten")* as well as the final stanza of "I have no peace" *("Meine Ruh ist hin")*. In general, Goethe often uses a six-line form of poetry (refer to the poem "To Well-wishers", "One and all", "Covenant" and others).

Thusly, both Goethe and Abai used the same rhyming schemes in their "hexastichs" – AABCCB.

Here is another example of graphic, structural similarity and stanzaic prosody, along with rhythm in Goethe and Abai.

On the left I will examine Mephistopheles song, as he sings to his own accompaniment on the harp, whilst on the right – a stanza from a poem by Abai *"Ем таба алмай"*. All presenting the reader with an opportunity to (at least visually) compare both forms:

Was machst du mir	*a*	*4*
Vor Liebchens Tür,	*a*	*4*
Bei frühem Tagesblicke?	*b*	*7*
La(I, lap es sein!	*c*	*4*
Er la.pt dich ein,	*c*	*4*
Als Madchen ein,	*c*	*4*
Als Madchen nicht zuriicke.	*b*	*7*
Босқа ұялып,	*а*	*4*
Текке именіп,	*а*	*4*
Кімді көрсем, мен сонан,	*б*	*7*
Бетті бастым,	*в*	*4*
Қатты састым,	*в*	*4*
Тұра қаштым	*в*	*4*
жалма – жан	*б*	*3*

For the same purpose – another fragment from "Faust" (the chorus of spirits) and two *«Сен мені не етесің»* ("What are you doing with me?) need comparison. Please pay attention to cross-talk as well as the external similarity of the rhythm.

On the right of the columns I will point out – as in the previous example – the number of syllables and rhyming schemes.

W eh! Weh!	*a*	*2*
Du hast sie zerstort,	*b*	*5*
Die sc hone Welt,	*c*	*4*
Mit machtiger Faust;	*d*	*5*
Sie stUrzt, sie zerfallt!	*c*	*5*

Ein Halbgott hat sie zerschlagen!	e	8
Wir tragen	e	3
Die Trümmern ins Nichts hinüber	f	8
Und klagen	e	3
Vber die verlorne Schone,	g	8
Machtiger	h	3
Der Erdensohne,	g	5
Prashtiger	h	3
Baue sie wieder,	f	5
In deinem Busen baue sie auf!	i	9
Neuen Lebenslauf	i	5
Beginne	j	3
Mit hellem Sinne,	j	5
Сен мені не етесің?	а	6
Меңі тастап,	б	4
Өнер бастап,	б	4
Жайыңа	в	3
Және алдап	б	4
Арбап	б	2
Өз бетіңмен сен кетесің.	а	8
Неге әуре етесің?	а	7
Косылыспай,	г	4
Басылыспай,	г	4
Байыңа	в	3
Және жаттан	д	4
Бай тап,	б	2
Өмір бойы қор етесің!	а	8

I fear, however, not every reader will have their interest kindled by such meticulous work. Therefore it is reasonable to limit myself to these given examples.

Anyway, is it permissible to ask: what's the use of such comparisons? What do they prove?

Of course, I cannot claim that in search of new rhythmic and melodic possibilities for Kazakh versification Abai relied on the experience of Goethe, or that he literally imported the stanzaic prosody and rhythm schemes of Goethe - after which he mechanically transferred them to the Kazakh language.

Rather, I am trying to show that Goethe and Abai were "attuned" in an almost "harmonic" manner. In their searches and experiments they spontaneously, or subconsciously – even though independently – arrived at the same goals and objectives. That they walked side by side along a similar path and achieved almost identical results.

An evidence becoming ever clearer.

* * *

Please remember, I am not writing a detailed study, but an essay. Something concise, with a purely informative mission. Hence, I confidently share some of my insights with readers: simply holding an open discussion on the subject of Goethe and Abai.

Any reader, of course, will realize I cannot innumerate all possible analogies within works by Abai and Goethe – similarities in motives, situations, typological parallels, philosophical, ethical or aesthetic attitudes. Assuredly, one small essay cannot reach the rigorous research required to fulfill this task.

In which case, let's imagine (at least approximately) what areas future researchers can explore?

Certainly, their aesthetic unity springs to mind, as well as cross-talk and the consonance of spirit and ideas.

"... the art of seeing a man is a rare art", - as Viktor Shklovsky observed in one of his works.

This is true. We do not always see those whom we meet almost every day for decades.

One of ways (and the most fruitful one!) for acquiring an additional comprehensive knowledge regarding Goethe and Abai would be comparative reading: undertaken to identify their views on the same topics, such as morality and aesthetic categories.

This can be called associative coupling between perceptions of world structure, as well as the duties of an artist.

All subtle issues, but ones revealing the spiritual affinities of Goethe and Abai within their respective timeframes As he says in "Maxims and

Reflections": "A human is always more or less the organ of his time". And again: "The greatest people are bound with their age by weakness".

Looking back, Goethe was in the midst of a turbulent era. A truth precisely expressed in his social and political worldview, as well as his creativity and practice. Hence, Goethe soon understood his remarkable spiritual mission, along with the impulses and physical efforts required to achieve it. As such, he authored the definition: *"des Lebens Leben — Geist"*— "The life of life is spirit". A saying inspiring N. K. Roerich to comment: "But it is significant to see how Goethe, as a genuine ambassador of the Truth, did not shy away from life, but found a smile for all of its colours. Restriction is unbecoming for the spirit that encompassed everything".

Yet, Abai too was a son of his age. His anxiety and pain reflecting the collapse of feudal and patriarchal society across the steppe. All giving birth to capitalism, something Abai immediately grasped. A realization determined by Mukhtar Auezov himself:

"All his life he suffered from scoundrels", despite the repeated complaints of loneliness. As such, he was well aware of his importance as a poet, as a person, as a citizen, as a humanist philosopher.

> *I walked the roads of being,*
> *with ignorant I struggled,*
> *And here I am at the peak...*
>
> *(interlinear translation)*

This thought is succinctly expressed in "Abai's Way": "The people waited for their poet and defender. Exhausted and unhappy people. His birthplace was as wide as the desolate steppe. Indeed, his lonely auls are lost in the vast desert. There is no permanent homelike place. No cities, full of life. Instead, are those scattered across the steppe, like a pitiful handful of baursaks[34] , scattered by a stingy hostess on a wide tablecloth... there is no trace of it, and no good. As the foam on the lake: arises and disappears. Today

---

[34] A type of fried dough food, found in the cuisines of Central Asia, Idel-Ural, and Mongolia. It is shaped into either triangles or sometimes spheres.

in a hollow, tomorrow on the hill… But where are the traces one can be proud of? Where is the inheritance for descendant people?.."

It seems that future research on the "Goethe and Abai" theme should go further along this way.

Undoubtedly, after two centuries of studying Goethe's work it seems everything about his life is known - albeit superficially.

Critics commenting he was born "in the afternoon, with the twelfth stroke of the bell" and to the throes of pain, ailing. A weak boy, although descended from remarkable ancestors like the German painter of the 16th century Luca Cranach. Uncannily, Goethe completed "Faust" just before before his death and exactly on 22nd of July, 1831, and so on.

Yet, it seems to me that in the fantastically ornate world of "Goethe Studies" there are still black spots in the philosophical, historical, aesthetic, ethical and cultural spheres, which can be defined as "Goethe's relationship to the East". To judge by suspicions for a moment, this great "spiritual continent" (as they called Goethe), is not disclosed by either his life or work. Rather, clues must be unearthed within his literary and artistic environment, of his epoch - inside the whole of Western civilization as a multidimensional phenomenon. All meaning, it is equally necessary to know the philosophy and poetry of the East, whose life-giving blood vessels also nourished the spirit of this "great Weimar dweller" – along with the brightest, colourful, sensual, world of "Morgenland" – where (according to the words of the poet), "in clear, wise style the mortal had a conversation with God and acquired the light of heaven on earth - a word without pain: without torments". Unarguably, to truly know Poetry, one must also read Hafiz, Jami, Saadi, Ferdowsi, Navoi and other stars on the eastern horizon

On the other hand, when studying Abai, it is necessary to identify the finest threads that linked his inner world, his strivings and pursuits in Western civilization, with its philosophy, history and social conjectures. It is no coincidence that he studied European economists and social scientists and got interested in the history of European social thought. Thence, he surprised the American traveler J. Kennan by asking him about his inductive and deductive method of learning. Clearly, the man, who carefully read Chernyshevsky, Dobrolyubov and Pisared, reasoned in complex philosophical categories,

Moreover, he was perfectly aware that numerous Russian Hegelians, Kantians, Schellingians, Fichteans, had left a significant mark on Russian culture. Undoubtedly, Abai, constantly communicated with exiles such as Michaelos, Bleck and Gross, Dolgopolov. Additionally, Abai had absorbed reams of material from classical Western philosophy. A phenomena evidenced reading his "Gakliya". It is felt by researchers in these elusive fields that telling discoveries await at the crossroads of two main routes – "Goethe and the East" and "Abai and the West". However, these topics will require extensive knowledge and laborious searches.

Regarding public views of Goethe and Abai - certainly similar motifs have long been intuited - stemming as they do from a sense of environmental reciprocity and historical mission. In this, one should especially emphasize both Goethe and Abai are beings resistant to usual time frames.

One may say they are never in the past. Also, they are always the contemporaries to their descendants. Here lies their greatness and immortality.

By the way, this is what Johannes Becher talked about: "We turn regard of the past to comprehend the creations of Goethe. But, having met his gaze, we feel like we need to rise up on wings, and fly from the past and through the present, while looking into the future - where his creations will gain their true impact: where his ideals will materialize. For the most significant feature is Goethe's comprehensive humanity - which lies in the future"[35].

The same idea was more succinctly put by J. Becher in his passionate and heartfelt speech in connection with the 200th anniversary of Goethe's birthday: "… A kingdom, called Goethe, lies in the future"[36].

It would not be a sin against the truth, I think, if we made interchangeable the name of this German national genius with the name of the great Kazakh poet-philosopher: since both passionately strained towards the future.

* * *

---

[35] Becher I.R., "On literature and art". Moscow, "Imaginative literature", 1981, p.87.
[36] Ibid, p.102

Any future researcher will finds abundant material for comparing the lyrics of Goethe and Abai.

In his lifetime, Goethe was recognized as one of the greatest poets in world literature. As J. Becher said: "Goethe was not only a profound lyricist, endowed with all the melodies of the human soul, from pathetic explosions, ecstatic hymns to the eloquent sighs of silence and whispers of the folk song…"

Furthermore, as A. A. Anikst emphasizes: "The very amount of his lyrical work is striking: about a thousand poems, about thirty five thousand lines, not counting great epic poems and verse drama. There is no form of poetry, in which Goethe could not have created masterpieces, each in its own way"[37]

I cannot say, how many lines of poetry were written by Abai, but it is obvious (without counting) the quantity is many times less than that of his German colleague.

In the book of "Myrzakhmetov, Mukhtar Auezov and problems of Abai studies" (in the Kazakh language) it is indicated that two hundred and thirty poems belonging to Abai, have been found (refer to p.132). It is also clear the point is not the number of lines, but the extent of Abai's diverse, comprehensive and rich lyrics.

His whole range - all shades of human feelings - are reflected in extant manuscripts. Hence, I do not think it is very difficult to illustrate this point with specific examples.

Let us take, for instance, similarities in understanding the poetic word in works by Goethe and Abai.

Constantly thinking about the social importance of words, poetry and art, Abai additionally mused on the role of a poet in the formation of public and national consciousness. He even outlined his understanding of this issue in his programme poems "Poems – the king of words, verbal selection" and "I do not write poetry for fun" as well as "Everyone goes to the bazaar, as I can see",—

These are the kinds of philosophical memes he penned on the nature of art in speech - as well as its meaning and purpose.

---

[37] In the book "History of foreign literature of the XVIII century" by Artamonova S.D. and Grazhdanskaya Z.T. it is said: "During his life, Goethe wrote about 1600 poems". (M, Uchpedgiz, 1956, p.358).

As we know, Goethe repeatedly appealed to the underlying theme of art. He always stressed the high importance of truly poetic words.

> *As in front of the sun — the darkness of the night melts*
> *In front of the power of a fiery word.*
>
> (interlinear translation)
> ("Ilmenau", translation into Russian by Levin V.)

Abai seems to echo him by saying:

> *The heart warms up, if the speech is mild,*
> *And the ear is caressed by the beauty of expressions.*
>
> (interlinear translation)
> (translation into Russian by Zvyagintseva V.)

In "Octastich" he also states:

> *Many-sided, flexible language,*
> *You are great in the mouth of the people.*
>
> (interlinear translation)
> (translation into Russian by Ozerov L.)

The life-giving creative power of the Word was repeatedly emphasized by ancient oriental poets. Their traditions, their understanding of the role of poetry reflected in the works of Goethe and Abai. Jami, who was highly revered by both Goethe and Abai, wrote:

> *Life of treasures is transient.*
> *And the price of words is eternal, I say.*
>
> (interlinear translation)
> (translation into Russian by Shamuhamedov A.)

Of course, this is about the true, sublime, spiritual Word, "golden on the inside, silver outside", according to Abai. Indeed, such words belong to the poet, "psalmist", who had cognized the magic and the mystery of this "king of words". Yet, it is also necessary for these words to be appreciated by listeners and readers.

> *Where is that guardian of the word,*
> *That comprehended the value of the Word?*
> – asks Goethe in his poem "Disclosure of the mystery".

This is the same question endlessly asked by Abai:

> *Who listens to the sensible word now?*

A frequent phrase in his poetry and prose being - «*сезді угарлық,*» — "the one who understands the words" is full of bitterness.

Goethe frequently tells us about a poet who is free and independent. Someone who protects his human dignity: like the writer in his ballad "The Singer". A wandering singer visiting feudal castles, wherein his songs amaze the king. Following which, he invites the singer to his luxurious, rich palace and offers him a golden chain as an expression of his gratitude. However, this royal gift does not entice the singer. To him, his freedom is the most valuable thing. So, the singer compares himself to a free bird that does not think of reward for singing. Indeed, he becomes weary of his position as a courtier.

With bitterness Abai also speaks about those akyns, that squander "the heat of their souls for a miserable pittance, pleasing everyone who comes along with flattery", while forgetting the true vocation of high poetry. Such people weave empty verbal patterns and achieve only intermittent fame through insincere praise.

> *The sounds of ringing strings were growing cheaper,*
> *And the thirst for songs in people was growing scanty.*
> *(interlinear translation)*
> *(translation into Russian by Zvyagintseva V.)*

True poetry, by contrast, has lofty aims and noble tasks.

> *How the song should be fed,*
> *In what should be the power of poetry?*

So that poets hearkened to it
And the crowd would learn it?

Goethe asks, and answers:

Firstly we invoke the love,
So that the song would breath it,
So that it would sound with sweetness,
And admire heart and ear.

****

Finally, with passionate heart
Seeing evil, we shall rail,
For we are friends with the beautiful,
But the enemies of the ugly.

(interlinear translation)
("Poems", translation into Russian by V.Levik)

This is how Abai understands the meaning and value of Poetry. Indeed, he claims, "I make verses not for fun, I do not fill verses with fiction". Instead, addressing his poetry to the young, with "sensitive ear, heart and souls" and to those whose heart is perspicacious and mind spotless. As a poet, he tirelessly appeals to goodness, generosity, love, sublimity, beauty, wisdom and honor. Feuding with the ugliness of life - for which Abai had exact names – lies, slander, boasting, sloth, covetousness, depravity, knavery and ignorance.

The gift of a poet is a rare gift.

Mortals equally seek verses,
But only the chosen is crowned with glory,—

(interlinear translation)

said Abai.

Unquestionably, Abai called those "singers" fools that "compose verses out of garbage": appealing to these "brother-chanters" not to empty words in his soul.

Reveal only the religious fervor, artist!
Work evenly, steadfastly, —

(interlinear translation)

– urges Goethe in the poem "Nature and Art".

As such, Abai raised Kazakh poetry to a new qualitative level. He understood the old akyn poetry had outlived its usefulness.

And if the speech of a singer is polluted
By words that are alien to the native spirit,—
Such song the world does not need,—

he says.

The time of new songs, new words had come. Abai calls the poems of his predecessors, famous poets of the 18th and early 19th centuries Shortanbay, Dulat, Bukhara-zhyrau the writers "of scraps and patches". However, Abai has some doubts - will his meaning be understood in the steppe? Is it accessible for everyone? He speaks about these suspicions in his poem "Everyone goes to the bazaar, as I can see". The initial lines of this poem in linear translation are as follows:

Everyone goes to the bazaar, as I can see
And one finds there whatever he is looking for.
One buys grain, another - corals,
Bazaar doesn't give everyone the same.
Everyone is looking for what he needs
And obtains what is within his pocket.

Abai is convinced the written word would not be lost; there will always be someone to pick it up, find it and give it to another.

What is meant here, in essence, is the difference between true and false poetry: the separation betwixt deep, intimate words marked with the sign of an artist and linguistic mundanity. With an ironic smile Abai adduces: "Why would a dog need corals".

In Goethe's poem "At the market" there is a similar ironies smile. Additionally, his poem narrates an imaginary debate between a true Master and his antipode: one who imagines himself to be an artist.

> *Today everyone has learned*
> *that any cobbler*
> *Whatever and however he stitches —*
> *He is already an artist!*
>
> *Well, give me rotten goods!*
> *Thus you will deceive yourself:*
> *You bargain off – that's what the market's for!—*
> *But you shall never be the Master.*
>
> *(interlinear translation)*
> *(Translation into Russian by Zakhoder B.)*

Themes transparently occupying each of these titans of verse. As we may read in Abai,

> *I write not for one person, but for the people.*

A similar idea was expressed by Goethe in his conversation with Eckermann: "By the way, someone who does not expect to have a million readers should not write at all".

The poet entrusts sacred materials to his verses. They are his soul, his pain, his joy and emotional turmoil.

> *But the hardest part is to hide a verse…—*

confesses Goethe:

> *But one should not repent poems anymore:*
> *Poems cannot keep secrets. -*

echoes Abai.

As such, conversation between the theater director, the poet and the comic actor in the Theatrical Performances of Goethe's "Faust" contains related themes. Indeed, each of these three characters sharply (sometimes even rudely) expresses his individual understanding of art and its purpose in life. Replicating the Poets creativity as touching a sublime, perfect kingdom, "peaks, where God's hand created the abode of dreams, the sanctuary of peace". All provoking the Actor to contend: "Rake off right from the thick of life".

For him, art is a "spark of truth amid the darkness of delusion". In the Theater Performance itself, Goethe, deliberately juxtaposes different opinions to express his understanding of the role of art and the place of a poet in social life. Many of which resonate with the basic views of Abai on creativity: on the role of Realist art and on the poet as spokesman for man as educator and herald of higher impulses, aspirations, as well as truths.

* * *

Nature always takes a pride of place in Goethe works. Primarily due to the fact Goethe was a follower of Spinoza - who claimed "God is nature". In Poetry and Truth Goethe admits: "At long last, I began to regard my innate poetic talent as nature, all the more so, as now I revered external nature as the object of poetry". Goethe praised nature solemnly, spiritually, and as an interaction of Life, with the Human. In Goethe's corpus nature is the epitome of beauty and freedom.

> *And here I drink new blood, fresh food*
> *From a world so free, so blest;*
> *How sweet is nature and how good*
> *Who holds me to her breast!—*

writes Goethe in his poem "On the lake".

One of Goethe's favorite ideas – drawing Man to Nature, or in other words, the desire of a man to merge with it became an endless source of delight to him. Evoking jubilation to the extent that in "May song", we may read of "the stream of energetic happiness" really seethes..

> *Wie herrlich leuchtet*
> *Mir die Natur!*
> *Wie glanzt die Sonne!*
> *Wie lacht die Flur!*

Es dringen Bluten
Aus jedem Zweig
Und tausend Stimmen
Aus dem Gestrauch.

Und Freud und Wonne
Aus jeder Brust.
O Erd, o Sonne!
O Gluck, o Lust!

How gloriously gleameth
All nature to me!
How bright the sun beameth,
How fresh is the lea!

White blossoms are bursting
The thickets among,
And all the gay greenwood
Is ringing with song!
There's radiance and rapture
That nought can destroy,
O earth, in thy sunshine,
O heart, in thy joy!
(Translation into Russian by Globa A.)

For Goethe nature is a personification of joie de vivre, the happiness of earthly life. It is the essence of life-affirmation. This feeling and understanding of nature Goethe conveyed in Faust, when thanking the spirit of the Earth:

You gave me Nature's realm of splendour

Equally, Goethe asserted that "whole-motherly nature… grants a man sense of eternal and infinite". For Goethe nature was synonymous with sincerity, chastity and charm. Confessed so, Goethe knew how to paint nature with the help of just a few exact, expressive strokes.

Here is the example of such depictions:

> *'Neath the waves are sinking*
> *Stars from heaven sparkling;*
> *Soft white mists are drinking,*
> *Distance towering, darkling,*
>
> *Morning wind is fanning*
> *Trees by the bay that root,*
> *And its image scanning*
> *Is the ripening fruit.*
> *(Translation into Russian by Levin V.)*

Indisputably, Goethe's pastoral poetry creates the feeling of youth, firmness, freshness, cheerfulness and bliss. I shall recall the opening lines of the poem "May":

> *Light and silv'ry cloudlets hover*
> *In the air, as yet scarce warm;*
> *Mild, with glimmer soft tinged over,*
> *Peeps the sun through fragrant balm.*
> *Gently rolls and heaves the ocean*
> *As its waves the bank o'erflow,*
> *And with ever restless motion*
> *Moves the verdure to and fro,*
> *Mirrored brightly far below.*
> *(Translation into Russian by S. Solov'ev)*

But a depiction of "pure", "static" nature was not an end in itself for Goethe. The soul of a bon vivant did not recognize itself when imprinted inside a still life. Thusly, Nature in Goethe's works lives in harmony with the irrepressible human soul and reflects its inner world.

> *If the living mercury creeps down,*
> *So be the rain and storm,*
> *And when it rises for a tiny bit —*

The blue tent of the skies is high.
Sadness and joy alternate inside of us
When we are in excitement;
In the close space our heart
Immediately feels them.
(interlinear translation)
(Translation into Russian by Solov'ev S.)

For Goethe, nature is not a "thing-in-itself", not an Absolute, not a separate divine creation, albeit beautiful and sublime. Rather, Nature and Man and Love and Life. Nature is art – these are Goethe's favorite themes; these are the combinations in which he is inclined to perceive nature.

Ah! the Spring's fresh fields no longer cheer me,
Flowers no sweetness bring
Angel, where thou art, all sweets are near me,—
Love, Nature, and Spring.—

he says in the poem "To Belinda".

Goethe constantly emphasizes the creative power of nature. He says: "Nature gives ignition to the soul." One poem by Goethe in particular bears the name "Nature and Art". It is about the harmony of creation, the art and skill commensurate with the eternal laws of Nature.

Nature and Art, they go their separate ways,
It seems; yet all at once they find each other.
Even I no longer am a foe to either;
Both equally attract me nowadays.
(translation into Russian by M.Rozanov)

Similarly, in Abai's work, we find a number of poems dedicated to the description of nature in different seasons. Each describing the beauty of nature by resorting to fresh, bright colours and national images – which he finds sublime and pure of tone. In my opinion, the ideological and aesthetic foundation of pastoral poetry in Goethe and Abai is directly comparable. Essentially, Abai pioneered pastoral poetry in Kazakh literature as did Goethe in German. For Abai, nature is always material, concrete, realistic beautiful, local, and inseparably linked with individual people and with the social environment. As such, Abai not only contemplates the wondrous scenes of nature, but also paints a purely "Kazakh" understanding of these realities. Hence, the volume of purely pastoral poetry in the works of Abai is small, although deeply revealing -

"The hunter goes hunting with an eagle in the newly fallen snow", "Summer", "Autumn", "October and November – these two months", "Winter", "Bright moon in the windless night", "Spring". Yet, these "verse sentiments" (of a related form) abound in his books: extensively describing not only the four seasons in the steppe, but additionally disclosing a holistic worldview. Indeed, they reveal his ideological and artistic credo, his understanding of social and public problems amid the conditions of nomadic life. Undoubtedly, Abai understood the significance of his creative endeavors and was fully aware of the novelty of works devoted to depictions of Nature. Basing, presumably, his outpouring on an experience of Russian and European landscape lyrics. Each poem of Abai's clearly being a broad realistic canvas, full of concrete realistic details. Joy, excitement, gratitude, light and hope run through every line of the poem "Spring". It may be a little more restrained in expressing exultant joy than Goethe's "May Song", but is in tune with his world outlook, with life-affirming fundamentals:

> *World is filled with blissful joy*
> *It is endlessly decorated by the Creator!,*
> *The Earth nursed with its mother's breast*
> *Everything that conceived in her Father-Sky.*
> *(translation into Russian by Shubin P.)*

In Goethe's "May Song" "all the gay greenwood is ringing with song!", and in Abai's "Spring" — "songs, the sun and the wind, and bird's hubbub". In Goethe "how gloriously gleameth all nature to me!", in Abai: "How noisy are poplars in springtime!" Goethe: "The bird rushes to the space of heaven", Abai: "The blue sky is full of songbirds voices".

"May Song" glorifies spring, nature, love, happiness, life. All of these themes and motifs are embodied in Abai's "Spring":

> *How can one not believe in the grace of the nature-creator,*
> *when the world of spring is full of endless bounties?*
> *(interlinear translation)*

The character of "May Song" passionately appeals to his beloved"

> *And all my heart's music*
> *Is thrilling for thee!*
> *Be evermore blest, love,*
> *And loving to me!"*

In Abai's "Spring" the Earth-bride, impassioned, awaits for that date with the Sun-groom.

> *And now she is young and bright again,*
> *Burst out laughing and singing, as the blooming poppy.*
> *(interlinear translation)*

The motif of hope and simple human joys are heard in another poem of Abai, «Summer». Aul, situated on dzhaylyau[38] is a summer station evoking mental clarity and peace. His colours are surprisingly soft:

> *In summer, when the trees are shady,*
> *And profuse flowers bloom on the meadows,*
> *And on the wide river banks*
> *Nomad's camps noisily scatter,*
> *The grass of the steppe is so high*
> *That the backs of horses are barely seen...*
> *(interlinear translation)*
> *(translation into Russian by Zhovtis A.)*

---

[38] Summer pastures in Central Asia and in the Altai region, located in the mountains, on the surfaces of planations, as well as in the wide river valleys and hollows.

Yet, for Abai. nature does not exist by itself. It is densely populated with steppe realities: flocks of geese and ducks honking and crawling in the steppe. Young women, "showing the whites of their hands and bending languishingly", setting up yurts, herdsmen on dashing horses hurrying to the aul, young men hunting with birds of prey, while old men sit on koshmas[39]. Everything is concrete, dynamic, beautiful, real. Nature and man are shown interacting.

In other "landscape" poems, Abai, realistically depicts socio-feudal relations in the steppe.

Amazingly, a soft lyricism, enlightenment, and spiritual purity fill the short poem by Abai entitled "Bright moon in the windless night". It is the pinnacle of pastoral poetry in Kazakh national literature. Filled with rich, purely national colours, this miniature reaches universality due to its humanity, internal concord and emotion. Critics claiming it is a hymn to nature and love, a freedom of feelings and intimate human happiness. Like Goethe, here man and nature move towards an authentic harmony and merge with it. Here is the full poem:

> *Quite night, in the moonlight*
> *Ray in the water trembles slightly.*
> *Behind an aul in silence*
> *Rivers thunder with rocks.*
> *The leaves of a drowsy forests*
> *Talk between themselves.*
> *Covering the dark dreenery*
> *Dressing the earth to its toes.*
> *Mountains catch the distant rumble,*
> *Shepherds cry - in silence...*
> *To the date behind an aul*
> *You came to me.*
> *Courageous and gentle*
> *Beautiful like a child...*
> *Having come from very far,*
> *Breathing hardly.*
> *This was no place for words.*
> *I remember the pure sound of the heart*

---

[39] felted carpets made of sheep or camel wool.

In the moment when you
Clung to my lips.

(interlinear translation)
(translation into Russian by Neyman Y.)

The emotions in Abai's works echoing natural phenomenon, as shades compliment each other, or contrast one another. To illustrate my point further, I shall give a short poem by Abai in the original interlinear translation:

Көк ала бұлт сөгіліп,
Күн жауады кей шақта.
Өне бойың егіліп,
Жас ағады аулақта.

Жауған күнмен жаңғырып,
Жер көгеріп, күш алар.
Аққан жасқа. қаңғырып,
Бас ауырьт, іш жанар.

Colorful clouds, coming unstitched,
Sometimes pour with the rain.
All pining with melancholy,
You secretly shed your tears.

Renewing from the rain,
The earth, becoming green, comes strong.
From tears, devastating,
Headaches, and inside burns.

With this in mind, I would like to ask readers to recall the above poem by Goethe "If the living mercury creeps down..." and, after reading it, to compare it with Abai's "Colourful clouds coming unstitched..." Isn't the inner relationship obvious here? Isn't it consonant? Aren't these two poems proportional - reflecting the same mental state of a person in rapturous moments?

* * *

Love, of course, is a central theme in the works of Goethe - glorified sometimes youthfully, passionately and fervent. Occasionally enthusiastic and sometimes philosophical, but always as a force igniting the imagination! Goethe wrote about love from youth till his declining years. It is enough to recall his "Zezengeym songs", inspired by a love for Friedrike Brion, or his frankly erotic "Roman elegies", in which the motifs of ancient Roman poets were used, or for that matter the "West-Eastern Divan", since it was penned by a sixty-five year old poet charmed by Marianne Willemer. Finally, his lyrical cycle "Trilogy of Passion", in which a surge of emotion is interspersed with the sad motif of renunciation - an impossibility of happiness.

To Goethe, love is not an abstract concept, it the world, wide and comprehensive. Love itself is fundamental to all human beings. Among five basic concepts that contain the essence of life, - Goethe enumerated "primary words" *(Unworte)* – such as Demon, Fortuity, Imminence, Hope and Love. Furthermore, the world according to Goethe, "is beautiful in all its measurements, then the root cause of this beauty lies in the life-giving power of love".

> *Everything is dear to me: oh, if it were eternal!*
> *Through the brink of love all is forever dear to me.*
>
> > *(interlinear translation)*
> > *(translation into Russian by Levik V.)*

> *Top of the dream,*
> *Love is you!*
>
> > *(interlinear translation)*
> > *(translation into Russian by Mirimskoy I.)*

All comparable with Abai's: "True love is the beauty of life" and love as a "living light" that illuminates and runs through the whole of human life, filling it with meaning. This is also a favorite theme in Goethe's oeuvre. Indeed, he varies it again and again:

The world without love is not the world...
(translation into Russian by Volypin N.)

Or:

And all my heart's music
Is thrilling for thee!
Be evermore blest, love,
And loving to me!
(translation into Russian by Globa A.)

Love - life – initiate a renewal of the soul, love - happiness, love - "early morning of May, of life", love - bright light into the heart, love - the world in all its lush splendor, wealth and beauty. This is the main philosophical basis of Goethe's understanding of love.

The youth, as glad as in his infancy,
The spring-time treads, as though the spring were he.
Ravished, amazed, he asks, how this is done?
He looks around, the world appears his own.
(translation into Russian by Levin V.)

Goethe states: love is an act (its meaning and purpose), blending one with the beloved. Love is one of the cornerstones in Goethe's worldview, since it develops his idea of the dual unity. In the inescapable longing for this unity (experienced as depth comprehension) with "another being, like him" - essential values are gifted. Curiously, the very same idea of a dual unity is heard in Abai's lyrics as well: "true heart is the conjunction of two hearts").

Before her sight, as 'neath the sun's hot ray,
Before her breath, as 'neath the spring's soft wind,
In its deep wintry cavern melts away
Self-love, so long in icy chains confined;
No selfishness and no self-will are nigh,
For at her advent they were forced to fly.

(translation into Russian by Levik V.)

Love, therefore, is the supreme gift of fate, the apotheosis of happiness.

> *And yet what happiness it is to love!*
> *What a delight for me – your love!*
>> *(translation into Russian by Zabolotsky N.)*
> *And I am weakened by love,*
> *And love has made me strong.*
>> *(translation into Russian by Gritskova I.)*

Overall, the love poetry of Goethe is wonderfully rich and covers all the subtle nuances of this sublime human feeling from its shy glimmer, to an all-embracing gleeful passion, comprehending both joy and happiness.

Ranging, as his texts do, from the desired flash of heat, to suffering due to a loss of loves, "irreplaceable yearning soul".

In the above passages from Goethe - written in different years of his long life - we can see the ***Standpunkt***, of his love lyrics expressing his belief in love.

Likewise, the noble feeling of love in all its forms and colors is described in poems by Abai. And as such, their poetry is once again proved consonant. Indeed, for Abai, love is the great joy, happiness, purification of souls and harmony of the senses. It is the beauty of external spirituality and. "Life is empty without love". An affirmation almost exactly the same as Goethe;s when he states: "The world without love is so empty and dead". All reminding readers that

> *The one that lived without love*
> *Cannot be called human, -*

claims Abai.

Love is the holy fire of Soul. It is impossible to imagine life without it:

> *There is no biy without the mind,*
> *There is no house without the light.*

> *If there's no fire in the soul*
> *There's only darkness, but no sight.*

He then emphasizes:

> *Ғашықтық — қиын жол.*
> *The path of love is hard.*

Abai speaks about love with the wisdom of a mature man, evoking sincere, but serious, feelings with psychologically subtly.

Indeed, Abai became highly innovative in his composition of Kazakh love lyrics. Thus forming new types of versification such as, "the language of love is speech without words". Teaching, thereby, young Kazakh girls and boys to talk about intimacy with a poetic enthusiasm and a chaste authenticity.

Hence, phrases like, " "Oh, my heart, stop beating", "My soul is abased", "What do you do to me?", "You praise me so neatly", "A hand-thick braid on the back", but not the buffoonery is dear" – are experimental. In them, Abai seeks to give voice to his ideal of feminine beauty, while warning against careless attitude towards our finer feelings. So, Abai's works on love are closely related to Kazakh concepts of consent. Yet, as always, he appears to be addressing the young - "I am speaking to the hearts of the young: to impulses" - he teaches:

> *Ғашықтық, құмарлықпен — ол екі жол.*
> *Love and passion are two different ways.*

And also:

> *Well, if you love, then do it with all your heart!*

And again:

> *Your ardor I advise to hold back,*
> *On womanizer there's dishonor man.*

Or:

> *Do not get carried away by outer beauty,*
> *Do not give yourself to blind passion.*
> *(interlinear translation)*

Or again:

> *The passion flame turns into chilly ice*
> *With those who spend their life in changing wives*

This is pure Abai. By, praising love, he acts as educator and humanist. Perhaps, for him, love lyrics and public-enlightenment went hand in hand – although often merging, and complementing each other.

Such was the demand of his time and social environment.

By extension, it is interesting to inquire into the ideal of feminine beauty for Goethe. How did he envision it? History knows, of course, the women he loved. Indeed, they entered into the memory and consciousness of generations. Thus confessing, Goethe wrote, "I was writing love verses only when I loved". Assuredly, many poems were devoted to Friederike Brion – the daughter of a village pastor. So, in "Poetry and Truth" we read: "I composed a lot of songs for Friederike on familiar tunes. They would make a bulky volume; only few of them are preserved, and it is easy to find them among my other poems".

In the same book Goethe describes Friederike as: "Slim and light, she moved as if having no weight, with two thick blond braids that fell from her graceful head, which seemed too heavy for her neck. Her brilliant blue eyes looked boldly on the world; a little cute upturned nose drew breath from the air - as if there were no worries in the world". Simplicity, naiveté, naturalness - these are the features of the female image praised by Goethe. These features are also outlined in depictions of Gretchen from "Faust." She is beautiful, simple, sincere, trusting, shy and modest, pure and innocent. She dreams of love, while remaining faithful to the last breath. Obsessed with her feelings for Faust, she manifests herself as a woman of integrity, passion and determination:

> *My heart aches*
> *To be with him,*

Oh if I could
Cling to him,
And kiss him,
The way I wish,
So I might die,
At his kiss!

                    (translation into Russian by Holodkosvky N.)

Relatedly, Abai's ideal of feminine beauty basically derives from folk traditions. Outwardly there are well-known signs: black eyes (clear as a mirror), black eyebrows, scarlet-red cheeks, a whitish open face, a gentle white body, beautiful teeth, hand-thick braids on her back and a white neck. All attributes mentioned by Abai in various verses. As such, they have become a kind of aesthetic measure of female beauty in the Kazakh lyrics.

Braids as the darkness of the night
Over the dawn, over the river.
The forehead is broad, the sight is deep.
Open up your face!

Bright mouth – sweet honey,
Shine of teeth – like ice.
I have lost my peace,
Lovely glance burns my heart.

Sinuous figure and tall,
Bent by the breeze,
You are white, as snow,
You are gentle as a flower.

You are sad – the distance is dark.
You are bright – the spring for us.
Your laughter is the song of a nightingale,
The whole soul is full of it.

                    (interlinear translation)
                    (translation into Russian by Petrovy M.)

However, when describing the features of female beauty, Abai considers it necessary to warn ardent young men:

> *Do not be under the delusion of beautiful woman –*
> *Find out what kind of character she has.*

And also:

> *Female beauty conceals dangers,*
> *Being available for many philanderers.*

while he even names those features of character that, in his opinion, decorate women: dignity, intelligence, restraint and respect.

> *I praise that woman*
> *That knows your soul by heart,*
> *Heeds your every heartbeat*
> *And wants to give her life to you.*
> (interlinear translation)
> (translation into Russian by Gatov A.)

Humility, austerity and emotional isolation in a woman does not appeal to Abai. Instead, he sees lively and harmonious women as his ideal. In his works, women respond to the passionate confession of a beloved when speaking about secret desires, about feelings openly, but with dignity:

> *Көңілің тұрса бізді алып,*
> *Шыныменен қозғалып,*
> *Біз — қырғауыл, сіз — тұйғын,*
> *Тояттай бер, кел де алып.*
> *Тал жібектей оралып,*
>
> *Гүл шыбықтай бұралып,*
> *Салмағыңнан жаншылып,*
> *Қалсын құмар бір қанып.*

Since the soul craves for me,
Inflamed with fever by me.
I am a partridge, you are hawk, enjoy, having caught me.
I shall wrap you with soft silk,
Bending as a vine.
Having languished under your weight,
Let my passion quench.

(interlinear translation)

Isn't this a direct correlation between the ideals of feminine beauty in Abai and Goethe? Isn't the abovementioned confession of Gretchen in "Faust" consonant with Abai's "You praise me so neatly"? Subconsciously, I am aware that in penning the eternal themes of love it is not difficult to detect an interconnection (and harmony) betwixt the works by Goethe and Abai, along with the verses of all poets at every time.

Yet, feelings of love in Abai's work always considered morality. His tentative comments breaking new lyrical ground - as Mukhtar Auezov observed. Hence, in the preface to his one-volume collection of Abai's works, published in 1954, Auezov wrote: "For the first time in Kazakh

Literature, so clearly and from such a height, new attitudes to the family, parenthood, education and, above all, to women, were evolved.

* * *

I think, in connection with the theme of the previous chapter it is time to focus on the "West-Eastern Divan".

This style of poetry is prevalent in the East and clearly links the work of Goethe and Abai in thematic terms. So contested. I will limit myself to some personal observations.

Firstly, Goethe and Abai shared an admiration for philosophical, ethical, and moral teachings across the ages. In this, they both wanted to learn the wisdom of the human race. Indeed, such a stance marks their mutual worldview, as well as their spiritual temperament. Nonetheless, this artistic process did not end there. Rather, they remoulded these materials to allow this universalist voice to speak in a recognizable national language. This, probably, is what makes them close to all individual nations and humanity at large.

In itself, the "West-Eastern Divan" is clear evidence of this.

Undoubtedly, Goethe was always attached to the cultural and artistic heritage of other peoples. This is evident from the majority of his works. Let us take, for example, his ballads, not to forget "Faust" and numerous other dramas. After all, his ballad «God and the Bayadere" is based on an ancient Indian legend. Moreover, at the heart of "King of the Forest" lies the Danish ballad; "Fulsky King", while «Gypsy Song» had Romany roots. Furthermore, Goethe's "Mournful Song of the Noble Mistress, Wife of Asanaga" is a re-working of a Serbo-Croatian folk ballad, and so on.

Immediately, one recall's Abai's: story of his dastan «Iskander» as derived from ancient oriental legends, as well as and the Koran. Further, his "Masgut" – is obviously indebted to "Oriental legend" by Turgenev, whilst "Azim" is a poetic retelling of a chapter from the "Thousand and one Nights".

Be that as it may, the Muslim East also enticed Goethe. Let us recall the "Song of Mahomet," published in 1774. In those years, Goethe additioally worked on the drama "Mohammed", which remained unfinished.

Certainly, by 1814 Goethe had become acquainted with German translations of Persian poetry by Hafiz – the 14th century wizard from Shiraz. His poetry has stirred the soul of an aging Goethe, who felt a surge of new strength and a flash of inspiration. About this Goethe wrote in his "Yearbook" of 1815, calling Hafiz a beautiful, magnificent (herrliche) poet. In his "Yearbook" of 1816, Goethe mentions the "Divan" again and says he was busy collecting material for it. Yet, a curious confession by Goethe in the "Yearbook" of 1817 states he needs to get into the spirit of the East. So, he studied calligraphy, although without knowing Persian, it was Arabic that he carefully reproduced. Additionally, in the winter of 1818 Goethe continued to work diligently on the "Divan", studying ancient Persian religion and customs, Arabic poetry and grammar. In the "Yearbook" of 1820 Goethe writes that once again he had turned to the "Divan" and had penned one of its parts – "Book of Paradise".

I am mentioning this in detail to show the importance Goethe attached to his "West-Eastern Divan", a very unique, complex collection, that was not immediately accepted or understood by readers and which caused a controversy among scholars of literature at the time.

Needless to say, I shall not go into complex debates and subtle (and sometimes scholastic) interpretations in this essay. I'm interested, after all, in a contiguity between Goethe's and Abai's creativity and their shared themes and motifs from the ancient East. For it is obvious the passion Goethe felt towards the East edges him closer to Abai. Quite logically, one is led to a juxtaposition of ideas and sentiments.

It is easy to imagine, what attracted Goethe to the poetry of the East. The versified brilliance, sensuality and freedom, high spirituality, a charm for the world, harmony of the Spirit and the Word, the ardor of imagination, joyous, elegant poetic expressiveness, allied to an allegorical way of thinking, and so on.

> *To the purer East, then, fly*
> *Patriarchal air to try:*
> *Loving, drinking, songs among,*
> *Khizer's rill will make you young.*
>
> *There, in what is pure and right,*
> *Generations I, with might,*
> *Urge to depth of origin*
> *Where they from the Lord would win*
> *Earthly-worded Heaven-lore;*
> *They will rack their brains no more.*
> *(Translation into Russian by Levik V.)*

So it is said in "Hegira" - a kind of introduction to the "West-Eastern Divan" - and in these lines one can already feel a flight of the spirit: a youthful enthusiasm and zeal, a hope to "return to the roots of soul".

It is also easy to imagine Goethe's reaction to the life-giving scent of freedom in lines from sweet-voiced Hafiz. As he no dount read:

Song, be ready to splash – again, and again, and again, and again!
Drink your chalice – it contains the essence of dreams! – again, and again, and again, and again!
Friend, with the idol you sneak to sit in sweet conversation, -
I am awaiting for the call to kisses - again, and again, and again!

(interlinear translation)
(translation into Russian by Lipskerova K.)

Goethe probably reveled in such ringing, sparkling lines: such musical imagery, full of charm. Indeed he exclaimed:

> *No, Hafiz, to compare with you*
> *Is impossible for us!..*

For his part, Abai had always been accompanied by the great eastern poets. He even experienced enthusiasm for their creativity in his boyish years, when studying in a madrasah. It is to them - to Fizuli, Shams,i Sayhali, Navoi, Saadi, Ferdowsi, and Hafiz that Abai addresses his youthful poetry: asking them to support his endeavors. It is their poetry he imitated when describing beauty —"*Йузи — рәушан, көзі — гәуһар* "— "with a face like a rose, with eyes like diamonds". .Moreover, it is their meter and poetic rhyme he sought in his own poetic experiments. As such, these poets were closer to Abai than to Goethe. Closer geographically and psychologically. Thus, Abai absorbed their spirit. He understood and felt them "from within". And he did not have to – in order to feel their spirit –reproduce calligraphy - he used Arabic script all his life. This topic is cumbersome, however, with many aspects and nuances.

Nevertheless, in the works of Goethe and Abai several motifs from eastern poetry can be heard quite clearly.

In my opinion, one of them is revealed in love lyrics, which echo innumerable harmonies. Unsurprisingly then, the theme of love in the "West-East Divan" is permeated by eastern philosophy, eastern attitudes, eastern traditions, and eastern forms of expression. All assertions exemplified in the last chapter of this essay. For the time being, I will examine well-known illustrations of this fact. In the "Book of Love, Ushk-Nameh" and in the poem "Models", Goethe brings six amorous couples from famous works of the East - Rustam and Rudaba, Yusuf and Zulaikha, Farhad and Shirin, Majnun and Layla, Cemil and Boteyna Solomon and Temnolikaya – and, (giving them short introductions), he comments:

Anyone who has learned a lesson,
Knows love by heart.

(interlinear translation)
(translation into Russian by Parin A.)

Yet, amorous couples listed by Goethe (and the works from which they were taken), were widespread in the Kazakh steppe in countless variations and retellings, What is more, Abai knew the originals very well, which can be seen from his work.

In the "Book of Zuleika: Zuleika-nameh" Goethe says:

To live with the beloved in love and harmony -
Paradise — and there is nothing else I need.

(translation into Russian by Levin V)

which easily allies him with eastern poets who wrote about heaven and their beloved. Relatedly, Abdurrahman Jami, of which Goethe said "amazing purity and prudence are his heritage", is the author of the following ghazel:

Why do I need a paradise in the afterlifes gloom?
There is joy on the earth.
For Jami, paradise is there,
Where he can see you.

(interlinear translation)
(translation into Russian by Stershnevaya T.)

Similarly, we read from Goethe:

... and you and I are as one flesh.
Since you called me the Sun,
Then come, and entwined around me, Moon!

(translation into Russian by Levin V.)

These images - the Sun and the Moon, eternal companions of love, as well as the embodiment of male and female — tale an erotic expression in eastern verse. Decidedly, one can quote an infinite number of examples from the poetry of Hafiz, Jami, and Ferdowsi, in whose descriptions of love the moon and the sun are always present. Let us recall Hafiz:

> *Unbutton your dress,*
> *Moon, crowned with the Sun...*
> *Or, again in his works:*
> *Recall your slave Hafiz,*
> *My happy moon of love…*

And how are those images – of Moon and Sun – celebrated in the Kazakh poetry! There are dozens of examples!

Unarguably, the explicit eroticism of eastern imagery is visible in these lines of Goethe as well:

> *When from your love you're riven, rent,*
> *As Orient from Occident,*
> *The heart is through the desert sent -*
> *Our guide no matter where we are.*
> *Baghdad - for lovers - can't be far!*
> *(translation into Russian by Levik V)*

How many refined names, magnificent definitions and vivid metaphors are extolled by eastern poets! What ingenuity and imagination they showed! And Goethe is not inferior to those charmers, those mellifluous wizards, when they called their lovers: "All-beloved", "All-present One", «All-beauteous-Grown», "All-Alluring", "All-Playfull", "All-manifold", "All-colour-starry", "All-surrounding", "All-clear", "All-heart-expanding" and "All-instructive" finishing their poems this way:

> *And when through Allah's hundred names I go,*
> *From every one - an echo-name for you.*

When reading love lyrics from the "West-Eastern Divan" one can clearly hear echoes from the ancient creations of famous eastern poets. Such sensations remaining when one listens to the songs and poems by Abai, dedicated to love.

Jami says:

> *Life without love is not even dust, but the particle of dust.*
> *(Translation into Russian by Ismailov H.)*

In this, one may recall Goethe's: "How empty, how dead is the world without love" along with Abai's "Life is empty without love".

Ferdowsi says:

> *The one, who forgot the path of love,*
> *believe me, cannot be called a human being.*
> *(interlinear translation)*
> *(Translation into Russian by Banu-Lahuti C.)*

Then we immediately hear: "And the one who lived without love, cannot be called human".

As Saadi says:

> *Everything is beautiful about love,*
> *Whether it brings us sufferings or balm*
> *(Translation into Russian by Derzhavin V.)*

And Goethe comes to mind:

> *"Through the brink of love all is forever dear to me".*

Ferdowsi also saying:

> *Oh, the path of lovers in an endless path!*
> *(Translation into Russian by Derzhavin V.)*

And we hear Abai:

> *The path of love is hard.*

While Hafiz says:

Beauty does not belong to the one who is slender and tall,
but in the heart of the choice lays the source of earthly happiness.
(Translation into Russian by Derzhavin V.)

Afterwards, we recollect that Abai meant the same when he said: "Do not be under the delusion of a beautiful woman – find out what kind of character she has.

Whereas Hafiz says:

Yes, I understood: the language of love has its signs.

To which Abai echoes: "The language of love is speech without words". One can quote for eternity.

The poetic word, inspirationally pouring out of the heart, while bewitching a listener has long been highly revered in the East. Indeed, the magical power of words was glorified by all the great poets. Let us recall Ferdowsi:

What is more beautiful
Then the captivating tonality of the word?
It is enthusiastically praised by young and old.

Or:

The poet can be proud of the creation,
Which is endowed by mind's illumination.

Or:

Poet, since you are only able to be a father
Of bad poetry, then please – no longer bother.

One more:

Only the word can save your name, if it's important
About the word: you should believe, its omnipotent.

A great multitude of similar statements are found in the works of Jami, Hafiz, Saadi, and Navoi. Interestingly, this understanding of the word was also the philosophical basis of Abai's aesthetics. All positions equally adopted by Goethe. Isn't this his theme in "Hegira", with his soul rushing to the "world, where the mortal led a conversation with God using words which were clear and wise?" Isn't this what is said in "Faust": "But the heart will not attract speech to the heart, since it doesn't flow from your heart"?

Another obvious orientalism can be seen in the "West-Eastern Divan" when Goethe uses the ancient "Nazira" tradition: a method of uncovering the plots and themes of his predecessors in a new way. Fascinatingly, Goethe sounds like he is competing with well-known poets from the East in artistry, in the possession of a vivid metaphor, image, whimsical metric and refined rhyme. Extraordinarily, therefore, he enriched and diversified German poetic speech in this manner. An innovation particularly noticeable in the tone-painting and figurative structure of his poetry. All said, here he is fully correlated with Abai.

Numerous variations of the "heart" theme, the multi-valued image of the "heart" as a vessel of spiritual substance, along with the cult of the heart – are significant motifs within Goethe and Abai. To my mind, a traditional style used by eastern poets. A device, moreover, joyfully employed by Goethe on numerous occasions!

Abai too uses these stylistics in his poetry and prose, synonymizing it with such concepts as honesty, loyalty, morality, love, piety, sincerity, kindness and mercy. In the "Fourteenth Word" Abai wrote: «The most precious thing of a man is his heart. Certainly, the Kazakh concept of "courage" and "cowardice" were born from the word "heart". Batyr is popularly called "*жүректі*", meaning "horseman with a true heart", whereas a coward is called "*жүрексіз*", that is, "the person whose heart is missing". All the best human qualities, such as sympathy, compassion and humanity are born in a heart. Even haste comes from the heart. And there is no lie when the tongue is obedient to the heart, while if the tongue is lying, then, the heart is simply being deceived" (translated by S. Sanbayev). In the "Seventeenth Word" of Abai Force, Mind and Heart come into dispute, proving their importance and benefits. Thusly, the heart says, "I am the king of life. I drive blood through the veins; the soul dwells in me, because there is no life without me!"

At which point, lets recall Goethe called the heart "the most mobile, most changeable part of creation".

Everything true, real and worthy comes from the heart, - that is what Abai and his poetry inspires. This idea sounds clearly in Jami's work:

> *The language is interpreter, the words are slaves, the heart subdued*
>   *them boldly.*
> *The speech that we have uttered, was born by our heart.*
> *The whole world and all the visible around: the earth, the skies*
> *Are a small part of what the heart contained.*
> *All life manifestations, your anguish and your love*
> *All that is written with the pen — your heart created, feeling worried.*
> *It is a striking arrow, that was sent by the bow,*
> *The hand only helped us, but the heart was neatly pierced.*
> *(interlinear translation)*
(translation into Russian by Stershneva T.)

One more private and, probably, not quite serious observation that I'd like to share here, is when reading Goethe I constantly came across the digital designation of "five". Here he distinguishes five types of parables, there he divides his opponents into five groups; Goethe also marks out five "primary words".

Intriguingly, Abai also uses this number repeatedly. According to him, the heart has five qualities: justice, satisfaction, conscience, gratitude and compassion. In another poem, he names five reasons that lead the Kazakhs to strife and discord: restlessness, shamelessness, sloth, envy, gluttony. In another poem, Abai teaches:

> *Бес нэрседен цашыц бол,*
> *Бес нэрсеге асыц бол,*
> *Адам болам десещз...*

Keep away from the five evils,
Be closer to five virtues,
If you wish to become a human.

(interlinear translation)

Furthermore, he proceeds to enumerate the five virtues to which one should strive, as well as the disadvantages that should be avoided. Speaking of love, Abai warns: "A five day love is unworthy".

Is this a coincidence? Where are the roots of this quinary symbol?

Unquestionably, in the countries of the Middle East a special genre of literature "khamsa" – "quintuple" is well known.

Nizami was its founder. These traditions were further developed in the works of Amir Khusrau Dehlevi and Abdurrahman Jami. As such, five poems (51230 lines) constitute a "Khamsa" - a "Quintuple" of Navoi.

As Jami says:

Observe five important rules...

In work of Saadi we read:

You hit the drum in front of you five times,
If destiny has given you good wife!

(translation by Starostin V.)

And Hafiz says:

You've set up the tent for five days.
Having taken some rest, look around...
Faithful gardener!
If you wish to spend five nights with the rose.
With good news
About a friend, bring me at least five lines!

Yet, it seems there is a definite connection in these examples. Partly explaining Goethe's addiction to the number five, while Abai's infatuation can be explained, I fancy, by the influence of eastern poetry.

Tellingly, the poem "Five Properties" from the "West-Eastern Divan" continues:

> *Five things five others never let appear;*
> *You, to my teaching lend an eager ear!*
> *From a proud breast will friendship never spring;*
> *The viler-minded nothing kindly bring;*
> *A mischief maker greatness never gains;*
> *Enviers care not for the poor man's pains;*
> *In vain the liar hopes he'll be believed.*
> *Hold fast to this; by no one be deceived.*
> *(Translation into Russian by Levin V.)*

These very personifications feature throughout eastern poetics. For example, in a book by Yusuf Khas Hadzhibey Balasaguni "Kutadgu bilig" ("Knowledge , bringing happiness") – there is Justice, Happiness, Mind, Contentment. Whereas, in a philosophical sketch by Abai ("Seventeenth Word") Force, Mind and Heart argue with each other.

Now back to Abai. What negative qualities does he advise avoiding?

> *Осек, өтірік, мақтаншақ,*
> *Еріншек, бекер мал шашпақ —*
> *Бес дұшпаның білсеңіз.*
> *Gossip, lies, boasting,*
> *Laziness, wastefulness -*
> *Five your enemies, if you want to know.*
> *(interlinear translation)*

And here are five virtues, which, according to Abai, one should seek:

> *Талап, еңбек, терең ой,*
> *Қанағат, рақым, ойлап қой —*
> *Бес асыл іс, көнсеңіз.*

Zeal, work, thoughtfulness,
Moderation, goodness - think.
Five virtues, if you agree,

(interlinear translation)

This is the pedagogical, ethical, credo of Abai: the essence of worldly wisdom.

As such, lets listen to the advice of Jami:

Observe five important rules in your life,
And on the earth you'll see paradise:
In wordly matters do not pertube the mind.
Do not in vain go risking with your head,
Take care of your health as of rare treasure,
Live in prosperity, but do not be rich.
And let your leisure be shared
With a reliable and cordial friend.
(interlinear translation) ·
(translation into Russian by Derzhavin V.)

It is easy, I think, to feel the harmony between these three poets. I also see parallels suggested by Goethe's use of "slander", "false", "boast", "lazy" and "wastefulness" resonating with - "boasting" ("boasting is a considerable sin"), "vanity of the mob" ("vanity of the mob is to feel that its power is eternal"), "halfwits" ("idiots, half-humans everywhere squeeze and put pressure on us"), "fools" and "bouncers" - in "The Book of Discontent. Rensch-nameh".

However, the "Eastness" of this motif does not need special proof.

After all, "The Book of Thought, Tefkir-nameh», from which the poem" Five things» is taken, is mentioned by Goethe himself as "devoted to the practice of morality and wisdom of life, according to the oriental tradition and temperament". Thus. his "West-Eastern Divan" is original, unique. It is a mine of eastern wisdom, perceived and written by a Western genius. As such, one needs to get back to it again and again. It is full of mysteries, like everything truly great.

* * *

Many consonances of theme and motif can be found in Goethe's and Abai's discourses on moral and ethical issues – all of which must be discussed concretely and in detail.

The only thing that keeps me from this is my fear of overly extending this essay: my extended tasting (like a good wine) of sweet and rare subjects.

Nonetheless, isn't it curious to find such close relations between motifs in Goethe's ballads (especially those written during his period of friendship with Schiller: the so-called "Period of Weimar classicism") and the three dastans of Abai, known to us?

Also, isn't it curious to discover such deep comprehensive influences by eastern poets on the work of Goethe and Abai respectively? In my opinion, the theme of education in the work of Goethe and Abai holds a number of unrevealed secrets. When all said and done, the idea of education constantly worried Goethe. A concern dating from the time he was buldungsroman - "Wilhelm Meister's Apprentice" In trying to understanding Goethe "harmonic persona", therefore, the door to further investigation is left open. Undeniably, Abai consistently talks about this very same matter in his philosophical essays. Indeed, he clearly reflects on «толық, адам» — defined as an amoral person.

Unsurprisingly, he regarded literature and art in a similar fashion to the Enlightenment humanists of the 18th century. As G. Lessing in his "Hamburg dramaturgy" emphasized: the purpose of art is "to teach us what we need to do and what not to do; to acquaint us with the true essence of good and evil".

All the work of Abai, therefore, could be said to investigate this problem. Talking to his people confidentially and frankly, he tried to uncover their eyes to the true nature of good and evil. With his philosophical turn of mind Abai mused on the same burning topics as Goethe. He shared, in a sense, the kingdom of Goethe and the spirit of Goethe. In this, he twins the psycho-physical nature of Goethe. Moreover, as a Kazakh poet who was obviously close to the spiritual quest of Goethe's "Faust" his pursuit of the truth was tireless.

Still, it seems to me I will write in more detail about all of this as time allows the flowers of investigation to fruit.

Goethe, of course, developed stylistic maxims and reflections, short notes, observations and contemplations on both abstract and concrete topics - in the genre of aphorisms and honed philosophical studies. Now, the roots of this genre lie, probably, in ancient rhetoric: in the dialogues of Plato, in "Experience" by Michel Montaigne, and "Maximas" of La Rochefoucauld.

Abai also paid tribute to this genre. His "Gakliya" – short, stylistically honed, lapidary studies - a set of philosophical and ethical, sociopolitical, satirical and accusatory thoughts and expressions demonstrating his admiration.

Indeed, reading Abai's "Gakliya", one involuntarily feels and intuits his consonance with Goethe. Here are just a few examples:

"Ah, how poor is everything around us, the Germans!" – exclaimed Goethe in an interview with Eckermann.

"I see, how in this turmoil my people becomes petty year by year, and more immoral. It is hard to look at it", – complains Abai in the "Third Word".

Generally, loving their people and being aware that they belonged to its fate, both Goethe and Abai mouthed harsh truths about them. Dialectically, this is clear and understandable. Ironically, it is this very love that Lermontov meant when using the word "strange" - "I love the Motherland, but with a strange love." This strangeness was contained in his eager desire to see his people better themselves. That said, no one, noticed as sharply as Goethe all the negative traits in Germans: in the German environment, in the German "burgher" (and somewhat philistine) society he so mercilessly denounced. It will suffice to mention the image of Mephistopheles - spirit of denial and ruthless accuser! As well as reflect on the poisonous sarcasm there is in "Xenia" - written jointly with Schiller, which denounced German "misery" in its various forms.

In himself, Abai was equally seized by the spirit of negation. Looking around, he felt compelled to expose and castigate the numerous deficiencies and deformities, defects and squalor of his surroundings. To the extent his heart was forced to endlessly repeat «жоқ,», «жоқ», «жоқ»— "no, no, no". It is hard to count how many times in his poetry and prose Abai is heard expressing this mournful, desperate «жоқ,». "no". Indeed, he bemoans the fact no aspiration, no concept and understanding, no science, no conscious act, no friends, no sublime passion, no honor, no conscience, no worthy rulers (nor even "per se" bays), no "real murzas", no one "who cares for good deeds" can be located. Everything is bad, everywhere is no, no, no. Despairingly, therefore, Abai asks, «So about whom should one be sensitive on this earth, and whom to love?" ("The Twenty-Second Word"). Addressing his compatriots, he additionally said, "Let us leave aside the faith; we will not talk about what Muslim you are. Instead, I inquire whether you are human at all?" ("The Thirty-fourth Word").

Let us recall the couplet "German National Character" by Goethe and Schiller:

> *To become a nation —*
> *You hope in vain, stupid Germans,*
> *You should've start with becoming humans.*
> *(translation into Russian by Toporov V.)*

Or as another couplet in "Xenia" cries:

> *Poems for Germans?..*
> *Germans are distrustful, fearful and deaf.*
> *Knock on their window – they might open it.*
> *(translation into Russian by Toporov V.)*

Doesn't this theme obviously appear both in Abai's and Goethe's works? Assuredly, each of them complains about their people and the national character. Twin poets indicating very similar vices - causing pain and resentment in their sensitive hearts?

Goethe, in a conversation with his secretary, noticed that people who are poor in spirit (as a rule), are suspicious. "As if nature, good-hearted to all whom she deprived of the gifts of the highest order, in order to compensate for the loss bestowed on them, arrogance and conceit".

Abai expresses similar thoughts in "The Fortieth Word".

Goethe continuing: "In order that talent could successfully and quickly develop, the nation that gave birth to it, should be inspired and inclined to enlightenment".

Again, Abai eulogizes "What do we do to become an enlightened people?" ("The Forty First Word")

Going further, when writing about the difficulties and complexities of ruling the people, Goethe says: "A lot can be achieved by rigour, much - by love, but most of all – by knowledge of case and justice, regardless of personalities".

The same thought Abai, offers in "The Third Word" - his own version of ruling Kazakhs: relying essentially on knowledge of case and justice. Thence, in "The Fourth Word" he exclaims: «Mind and discipline lead to prosperity".

Reading Abai, or different studies about him, one can't help thinking: what a loss to us all. What a shame the great Kazakh poet did not have his own Eckermann - that he did not keep a diary, did not leave a detailed life story, or an expanded biography of his soul. Or for that matter, a plurality of explanations and clarifications on each particular occasion, as Goethe did! How much he could tell us, how many unsolved and probably impenetrable secrets could this outstanding man uncover. Goethe connoisseurs are lucky, it is much easier for them, Thus we can say that the farsighted, prudent, careful and scrupulous Goethe pretty much took care of everything himself.

Those things he did not have time to do himself, were professionally carried out by his secretaries - under his leadership. In his later years Goethe had six of them. «Some of them, having mastered quite well the everyday style and handwriting of the writer, produced "handwritten letters of Goethe" quite often (N. Vil'mont).

Of course, Abai also had students - educated young men, History knows tham as Kokbay, Murseit, had Kakitay ... But a deep and true understanding of his work, its place and importance in the national culture, was not widely determined during the poet's life, or for decades after his death. Indeed, little information about Abai had leaked to the pre-revolutionary Russian press. It is hardly surprising then that literary references (usually confined to the archive of the Russian Geographical Society of 1901) are next to nonexistent. Only a review by local historian A,N,Sedelnikov in the book «Russia. Full geographic description of our fatherland «(1903), to the obituary in memory of the poet, published by Kakitay (1905), survives in full. Although, one may find in "Nasihat-Kazakiya", a prose translation of Abai's poems, made by S. Sabantayev and N. Ramazanov. Nonetheless, it is such a pity.

Regarding his "Maxims and Reflections" Goethe wrote out one of the thoughts of Aeschylus: "the intelligent have a lot in common".

This thought must have pleased Goethe: attracted his attention.

Another example of the creative harmony between men convinced of the truth.

Great men, dare we suggest, who have some kind of common "enzyme" of spirituality. Something usually expressed as unity, or a likeness of spirit amongst those committed to Truth, to Beauty, and to Life.

Similar paths, after all, should lead to a common goal, to mountain peaks.

* * *

To comprehend is to know, to understand, to feel the multifaceted creativity of Goethe and Abai - a daunting and inexhaustible task. Certainly, they must be read slowly, penetrating into every word, into the essence. For years. For all of ones life.

Reading is art. Reading is work.

In his book "Conversations with Goethe" J. -P. Eckermann records a story about Soret, a friend of Goethe's. Therein, we discover: "He (H.B. - Goethe) said a few humorous words about the difficulty of reading in general and about the arrogance of some people, imagining that any philosophical or scientific work can be read without the proper training (like the first available novel), - these fellows - he continued - do not even know how much time and effort it takes to learn to read. I spent eighty years, but even now I cannot boast that I have reached the goal". Such was the way one of the most learned men of his time educated Goethe.

That was the way a self-taught Abai read - thoughtfully, seriously, getting to the bottom of things consciously. This is perfectly clear from his philosophical studies "Gakliya", from his sensitive, extremely economical attitude to the word, from his entire artistic credo.

Analogously, Goethe and Abai should be read. Only then can one experience revelations of the human spirit. Only then can one feel the quivering joy of learning.

The works of Goethe (led by the immortal "Faust"), definitely do not present easy reading. Something that is meant for "swallowing on the go", for fun, for mindless entertainment. The same can be said about Abai. In creations by these poets one should be patient to grasp their meaning. Returning to them again and again when questioning life. These twin titans had the gift of speaking poetically and philosophically about things that excite a man's soul. As such, they challenge every new generation, despite temporal differences in world cognition.

We should also remember that both Goethe and Abai had a potent gift for absorbing, assimilating, processing and summarizing all that had been achieved by their predecessors and contemporaries. It must have been this feature of comprehensive intelligence, which Klopstock referred to when calling Goethe a "powerful invader."

Goethe himself, however, said: "I have my works not only thanks to my own wisdom, but also thanks to thousands of people and circumstances outside of me, which gave me the material for them."

And on the same occasion: "My work was created by the collective being, which bears the name of Goethe."

I think, Abai could confess to the same fact. All his works show similar features of this gift.

Either way, Goethe and Abai are a concentration of national spirituality. It is equally possible – and more accurate – to say broadly: of all-human spirituality.

However, such attributes may be common to all the great poets.

Geniuses have a shrewd comprehension into those depths of life unknown to us and usually inaccessible in words: terms Abai named "сез патшасы» " - the kings of the word".

They lift us and open us to life, to the Spirit of life. They inspire us:

> *Who lived, shall not turn into nothing!*
> *Eternity is everywhere,*
> *Concern is blessed with being!*
> *It is eternal; and the laws*
> *Keep, firm and supportive,*
> *Pledges of marvelous changes.*

(interlinear translation)
(Goethe)

The nature is mortal, and humans are eternal,
No matter of he died or not – life doesn't stop.

(interlinear translation)
(Abai)

They give us hope and tirelessly urge:

Let your inquisitive eye
Tirelessly watch the creative flow,
Join the earth's chosen ones.

(interlinear translation)
(Goethe)

You can become a scientist.
Cheer up, the one with little faith!
Take the example of the greatest,
And never say "What can I do?!"

(interlinear translation)
(Abai)

They - the sages and philosophers - teach:

How creates he, invisible for the crowd,
His dear world with his will
Both contemplator and a poet,
The same you, the sacrament of grace,
Entrust your brothers highest gift,
And there is no better life for mortals!

(interlinear translation)
(Goethe)

All the mortals need success and goodness,
But we should separate good from evil.
Goodness, justice, are our friends,,
With them you shall step over the graves threshold.

(Abai)

What is the conclusion of these modest observations and the comparisons, recounted (mostly freely and fragmentary) in this essay?

It is too early to make conclusions.

So far one thing is clear. There are names that represent a whole country, the whole nation. When we hear the word "Italy", Dante instantly flashes into our minds. When we hear the word "England", we recall Shakespeare. The word "Germany" is inseparably connected with the name of Goethe, "Russia" – with Pushkin.»

All true Kazakh's fit into the rich name – Abai. It is like a symbol. The banner of a people on this planet of mixed multitudes.

As concrete as hard truth, so is the concrete of greatness and of the Great. Their specificity can be expressed in words. «The greatness of a poet - is that he serves as a source of inspiration to his people, strengthens the faith of his nation and feeds its pride. We can say a great poet extends the life of a nation. In broad historical ways. People's turn to the heritage of genius, falling before the crystal clear spring of its creative works, and drinking the water of life from it evermore.

Sentiments such as these were written by Konstatntin Alexandrovich Fedin in his article "Johann Wolfgang von Goethe".

Here everything is weighed, formulated concisely and precisely.

The great are consonant. They are spiritual brothers. They often talk about general matters, common to humanity. They echo each other through ages and distances.

And that is why they are clear and close to the mingled folk of the earth. Like Goethe and Abai are close and clear to each other. Like they are close and clear to us, their descendants - for the greatest poets of the past are the active participants of our modern cultural life.

Being a nine-year old child, in accordance with the curriculum I learned by heart (yet noticeably mangling Kazakh words), the poem by Abai "Winter" impressed me. The "old matchmaker, white old man" that "has done a lot of harm" became etched in my memory. His breathe being the reason for the cold, snow and storm.

There was war. A tiny aul on the bank of the Ishim River under the snow. A blizzard raging for weeks. So, sitting in the light of a weak seven-lined petroleum lamp, clinging to the blackened stove, I stubbornly repeated under the monotonous howling of the wind in the chimney: *«Ак, кимда, денелц ак, сацалды...»* and right beside me, cradling my freezing little sister, my mother softly sang: ***«Roslein, Roslein, Roslein rot, Roslein auf der Heiden»***, not knowing that this is a poem by Goethe. It was already about two hundred years since

"Little wild rose" became a German folk song. In the head of a school junior, two images had merged: winter, frost – "old matchmaker, white old man" and a beautiful rose in the open field, that, "having forgotten fear", the young man picked up unreasonably.

That was such a strange interweaving

Abai imperceptibly entered my soul, of course, in this language environment. Abai was studied in school. Extracts from the "Abai" tragedy were performed on the club scene. Abai's songs were sung by toys[40] and at parties. Abai's poems, sayings, aphorisms always intertwining with the speech of our auls' inhabitants.

Yet, somewhere in the distance Goethe, as an inaccessible, mysterious pinnacle, beckoned me.

Over the years they have become closer, dearer and essential to me.

They are always within reach. When reading Goethe, I certainly think of Abai. When reading Abai, I feel close to Goethe. In this, I am constantly happy and surprised. How close they are, how consonant, how akin! They are the personification of everything humane, beautiful, sublime and noble.

It is known that Tolstoy held a similar attitude. In his diary on June 2, 1863 he wrote: "I read Goethe and thoughts are swarming …" Goethe needs to be read for a whole life, he excites, stimulates the mind of readers of all ages, and now it seems me, especially in a mature reader that has known life. The same can be said about Abai. His poems and philosophical studies are familiar to us from childhood, They are constantly "heard everywhere", and yet, reading Abai, one finds oneself thinking that this or that line has highlighted something in a different way, in a new way. Completely, suddenly, one gets a grasp again and again, as if rediscovering it in different periods of life, gets a grasp, thinks about it… "…the thoughts are swarming".

> *If the eye wasn't solar,*
> *How could it see the sun then, -*
was written by Goethe.
   Both Goethe and Abai had solar eyes.
   Goethe and Abai…

---

[40] Among peoples of Central Asia: a holiday (wedding, circumcision, etc.), accompanied by a feast, folk entertainment, etc.

Peaks of poetry. Great satellites of objective reality. Mentors and comforters. Always and everywhere.

Learning and comprehending their work is like a holiday.

1986

CONSONANCE

Goethe's "Wanderer's Night Song" in translations of Lermontov and Abai

Essay

Sweet union since ancient times
Gets poets in-between connected:
They are the priests of single muse,
To single flame they are affected

Pushkin

Consonance… It is everywhere. In nature. In music. In poetry. In lofty and noble impulses of passion. In human hearts. In human speech.

There is consonance of the spirit. Consonance of talent. The unity of language diversity.

And that is the main theme of this essay…

… From somewhere in the steppes evening twilight approaches slowly and inexorably, gradually becoming thicker. Down there, along the Ishim River, over the impassable tugay[41], hangs thick darkness. Aul plunges into the night. Along with it comes the silence, deaf, viscous. But now everything is quiet, the silence is getting louder and louder, and shadows no longer glide – they are frozen, and one can hear how the shore water rubs on coastal pebbles and whispers something gentle at the ford Tas-Utkelov.

Slow lyrical song floats slowly from the last house on the edge of the birch copse.

Қараңғы түнде-е-е тау
қа-а-алгы-ы-ы-ып…

---

[41] a form of <u>riparian forest</u> or <u>woodland</u> associated with <u>fluvial</u> and <u>floodplain</u> areas subject to periodic inundation, and largely dependent on floods and groundwater rather than directly from rainfall.

The voice of the singer is growing, expanding, becoming filled with a tight power, ascending gradually, as if climbing the stairs,

In the dark night mountains, napping...

Slow, stately. the pace of the night in every word, in every sound of the song. Perhaps, back then, in the days of Abai, the great Kazakh akyn, this slow, sedate, song flew over aul in the Aksholky tract with the same "slow and smooth breeze as Sary-Arka". And people resting after a gruelingly long summer day in their yurts, listened to this creation of their wise, famous countryman, completely unaware that the words of the song came to the steppe from another world, unknown to them.

Indeed, isn't it a miracle that "Wanderer's Night Song" by Goethe captivated Lermontov by its elegance , and he, as Belinsky shall say later, "gracefully" translated it into Russian? And isn't it a miracle that after half a century, the son of the mysterious Kyrgyz-Kaisak steppes Abai Kunanbayev will recreate it - in his native Kazakh language in a manner, no less gracious?

Traveling over small and big countries, "Wanderer's Night Song" flew once «to the village in the tract Akshoky, from there to dzhaylyau of Tobykta, to uppers reaches at Kers[42], to Uaks[43], to the tribes Karakesek and Kuandik, to Naimans, inhabiting the Ayaguz valley, Tarbagatai Mountains and Altai «(M. Auezov "The way of Abai")

* * *

The old truth: the greatness of the great, as well as the beauty of the beautiful, like everything we can understand, realize, feel, explain only by comparison.

"... only the contact of one language with another on the basis of comparisons, - of how one and the same thought is differently expressed in different languages, - naturally makes us stop on the

---

[42] Ancient nomadic tribe, now part of the Kazakhs and Mongolians.

[43] Tribe, now one of the six tribes (Konyrat (hungirat), Uak, Kerey, Argyn, Kipchak and Naiman), constituting the so-called Middle Juz of the Kazakhs.

means of expression and makes people attentive to the subtle nuances of thought and feeling"[44],—said Academincian L.V. Scherba

Of course, it is interesting to trace (resorting to comparative linguistic analysis), how one and the same poetic idea is transformed when translated into different languages, especially if the original translations are owned by a famous artist. The famous Goethe miniature, translated by Lermontov and Abai, is fertile material for such a linguistic experience, the essence of which goes beyond a "purely" scientific sphere.

"Wanderer's Night Song" (*«Wandrers Nachtlied»*), written by Goethe on the night of 6th to 7th September 1780 with a pencil on a wooden wall of the wood house on the top of Kikelhan mountain ridge near Ilmenau - has been on the lips of many generations of different nations and tribes for two centuries. There is inexplicable charm and a magical attractive force within this tiny poem that worries and excites readers, artists, composers, research scientists, as well as literary commentators. There is something sublime and proud in the immortal lines, which inspired Abai and Lermontov to translate this work into their native languages. Something leading to the emergence of new masterpieces that marked a kind of spiritual connection of the poetic genius of the three peoples.

Uber alien Gipfeln 1st Ruh;
In alien Wipfeln Spiirest du Kaum einen Hauch;
Die Vogelein schweigen im Walde;
Warte nur, balde Ruhest du auch.

I will give a word for word translation, well aware that it, as always, destroys the beauty of the poem:

Above all the peaks
(There is) peace.
On every top of the tree
You can barely feel the breeze.
The birds are silent in the forest.
Just wait, soon
You will rest, too.

---

[44] Scherba L.V. Selected works on Russian language. M., Uchpedgiz, 1957, p.53.

It is desirable, of course, that a hypothetical reader would not glance swiftly, at perhaps, an unclear original text, but would read it a little more closely - going into its rhythmic pattern and rhyme. A lyrical miniature breathes amazing peace, bliss, universal tranquility.

It is obvious it is written in one breath. A text immediately leaping from a happy moment of inspiration. It is also clear that the "Wanderer 's Night Song" is a new stage in the creative evolution of J.W.Goethe. "The former rebel now strives for harmony and peace, which is especially reflected in the impressively beautiful « *Wandrer's Nachtlied*»,— writes the great Goethe connoisseur and scholar A. A. Anikst. Further expanding on the content of miniatures, he adds:" If the main idea of the poem is clear from the very beginning, the thoughtful reading of it, based on the knowledge of the views of the poet, his philosophy and spiritual quest, shows how much Goethe imported into meager lines of his poetry and how much attention is needed from the reader to comprehend the depth of meaning, hidden in some of the seemingly simple poetic lines. Indeed, the rhythm of the poem, its melodic structure evokes a sense of peace and harmony, which saturate the landscape described in the poem.

Although, curiously, it is not described. Instead, every word evokes the whole picture before a readers inner eye. This is the magical power of Goethe's poetry, combining thoughts, feelings and visual impressions as well as musical soundings"[45].

Peace and harmony ... The synthesis of thoughts, feelings and music.

In fact, even someone that doesn't speak German can catch fluency, sonority and the grace of phonetic instrumentation in this poem. Listen to these flimsy, soft "Cental European "L": «:allen, Gipfeln, Wipfeln, *Vogelein, Walde, balde:*, to this dull, lingering, as if aggravating the darkness of the night sound «U»: *Ruh, du, nur, ruhest,* to the mysterious and affectionate «O»: tiber, spiirest; pronouncing the word *Hauch* with a soft aspiration. Exactly the way "*h*" should be pronounced at the beginning of the word, making it sound like a whisper, like a subtle whiff, while together with «sch» («schwei- gen») and «ch» at the end of words — *Hauch, auch* it emphasizes the nights silence, spilled over the world.

---

[45] Johann Wolfgang Goethe, Gedichte, M., Progress, 1979, p. 13-15

What is this? Is this the picture of nature, sketched with one stroke by the hand of genius? Or an exquisite miniature, inspired by specific contemplation, personal experience? Or apparently something so simple, affordable and unpretentious that it is filled with a deep abstract philosophical sense? There are many interpretations of this masterpiece. People who had studied the life and work of this Weimar genius very well, eagerly sought in "Wanderer's Night Song" a deep-seated, latent context. Noteworthy is the interpretation proposed by M.S, Shahinian who wrote, "Goethe's "Wanderer's Night Song"... thinking maybe about his sister Cornelia, who died six years earlier? Seized by the picture of sleepy nature, he felt that he could not avoid the impending nothingness of the night. But for the one who imagined life as a continuous feat of labour, death seemed rest, inherent and essential to man, same as to nature - a kind of "expiration" after greedy "breaths" of life"[46].

It's hard to say whether Goethe's little poem was inspired exactly by these feelings, but it is possible to assume it. However, Goethe himself had a mocking attitude toward those who were looking everywhere for deep thoughts, or put deep thoughts and ideas everywhere. In a conversation with Eckermann, he said: "It is not in my habits to tend to embody abstract concepts in poetry. I always perceived sensual, sweet, colorful, manifold impressions of life and my vivid imagination eagerly absorbed them. As a poet I only had to artistically form and complete such, trying to recreate the vividness to ensure that they have had the same effect on others"[47].

Of course, the work of art is not a set of some beautifully expressed abstract ideas and formulas, and as a poet Goethe sought, above all, to convey in the living word his contemplations and experience. Yet, it was too big, deep and complex to be unequivocal.

In the "Wanderer's Night Song" a picture of the night is wonderfully reproduced, while the author has managed to convey to his reader its tranquility and majesty. But I think, in the subtext of this miniature we can clearly feel something more philosophically heartfelt. Something

---

[46] M.Shahinian, Goethe, M-L, ed. USSR Academy of Sciences, 1950, p. 34
[47] I-P. Eckermann, Conversations with Goethe, M., "Imaginative Literature", 1981, p. 534

poeticized, soulful and secret that gives it a special charm. After all, its power of attraction lies not only in the laconic imprinting of nature at night. Rather, Goethe remembered his journey (made when he was a much young man to the green hills of Thuringia), and aimed at making it accessible to everyone: a unique undertaking at the time. As such, it is probably not a coincidence that, fifty-one years later, (shortly before his death), Goethe relived this experience accompanied by his grandchildren.

As an elderly poet, he may even have thoughtfully whispered the last two pathetic lines of «Wanderer's Night Song" with tears in his eyes to those around him? At least this is how the anecdote goes according to Goethe connoisseur N. Vil'mont. Interestingly, he also writes, «Goethe read it to himself, and tears ran down his senile cheeks. «Yes! Thou, too, shalt rest", - he said in a touching voice. Then he paused for a moment, looked out of the window at the darkening forest, and said to his companion (Eckermann): "And now let's go".[48] How lovingly he describes this last journey in his letters to friends - Zelter (9.4.1831), Count Reinhard (7.9.1831), Louise Adele Schopenhauer (19.9.1831)! Obviously, the "Wanderer's Night Song" was born during a time of high spiritual tension: at a very important turning point of spiritual quest of the author.

It goes without saying Goethe is an amazingly complex spirit, combining a multitude of contradictory and conflicting passions and desires.

Maybe this is why his external, quite prosperous and respectable life (often overwhelmed by the impulses of invincible spirit and an irresistible thirst for action), did not coincide with his genius. Rather, he constantly strove for harmony in life and in soul, even though he only reached it in rare moments.

Let us recall Goethe's life at the time he created the miniature.

Goethe in those years was still young, but already the world-famous author of "Werther". Hence, he was a poet idol. Moreover, he was a courtier in a small Duchy; experiencing the power of government and taking the post of Minister for War and Public Works. Thus, he longed

---

[48] I-P. Eckermann, Conversations with Goethe, M., "Imaginative Literature", 1981, p. 16

for great things and, confident of his potency, took a lot upon himself, while being surrounded by fame and love.

Yet, this is only the superficial, visible aspect of his life. In fact, he had already lived through the multifaceted disasters inside Pandora's box: the bitterness of unrequited love, along with a sense of loss and frustration as a humanitarian. All causing a depression and vague anxiety regarding his future titanic struggle against intellectually narrow confines.

These tensions are clear in "Wanderer's Night Song", but had already surfaced in a work four years earlier. Here it is:

> *Thou that from the heavens art,*
> *Every pain and sorrow stlllest,*
> *And the doubly wretched heart*
> *Doubly with refreshment fillest,*
> *I am weary with contending!*
> *Why this rapture and unrest?*
> *Peace descending,*
> *Come, ah, come into my breast!*

The connection between the two similarly named poems by Goethe is manifest. They is expressed both in construction and, most importantly, in the tone, mood, and passionate plea: "Peace descending, come, ah, come into my breast! Not to mention in the sad consolation: "Wait; soon like these, thou, too, shalt rest". Is it difficult, therefore, to notice the close echo in lines "I am weary with contending" and "thou, too, shalt rest"?

Observably, Goethe (as Privy Counselor) had said farewell to his youth. Cooling, thereby, his bygone passions.

Anyway, they had pained him. As had the alienation which had taken place from his friends. All developments making Goethe increasingly withdraw. He admitted: "Sometimes my legs fail under the unbearable weight of the cross ,that I have to bear almost alone" Increasingly then, he dreamt of a sublime peace. His love of women not having brought him any harmony. At times, he even seems to experience premonitions of death. A byproduct, possibly, of the continual inconvenience Werther delivered into his life. Tellingly, these signs and marks are present in

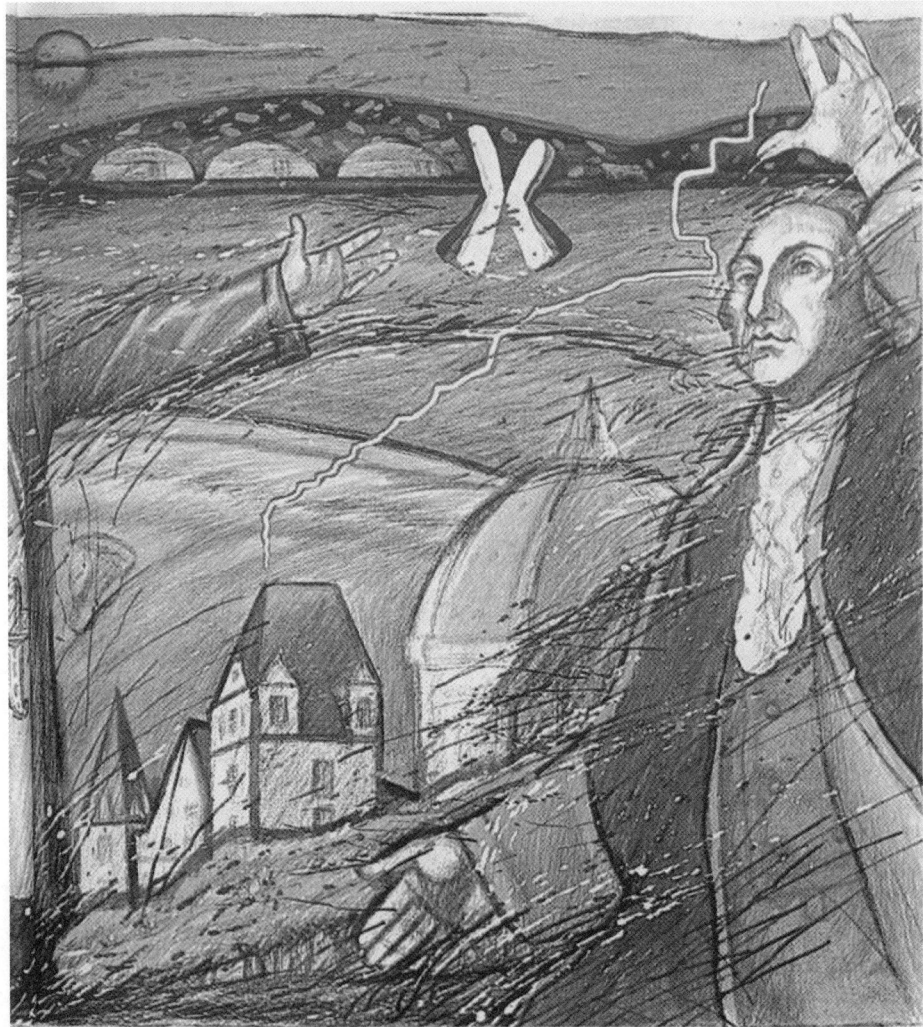

Clower's sculpture of Goethe. Indeed, this remarkable piece shows the poet at thirty years of age. Curiously, its overly tired face appears much older, while its sadly depressed lips reveal a trace of mental anguish and suffering. Time had noticeably extracted its due.

Maybe in the mountains, "the final conclusion of the wisdom of the Earth" could offer release? Either way, this master will eventually uncover his thoughts in the main work of his life – "Faust".

Maybe that night the idea of a higher purpose in mankind came to him, compelling him to exclaim: "Moment, stop, you are beautiful!" On the other hand, perhaps, he had a presentiment of what a titanic work was coming, and recognizing this, he consoled himself by saying: "Thou, too, shalt rest..."

Maybe... maybe...

* * *

These well-known words have been transparently reflected in almost every translation of this miniature. Especially in transcriptions by made by Lermontov and Abai. Although, these are not translations in the usual sense, but rather a competition on equal terms between two great poets to achieve spiritual consonance.

Consonance of talents, dare we say? A unity in language diversity?

As such, everyone remembers Lermontov's childhood lines:

> *Tops of dreaming highlands*
> *Darken in a night;*
> *Valleys lull, in silence,*
> *A fresh dim inside;*

> *Warte nur, balde*
> *Ruhest du auch...*

> *Wait; soon like these*
> *Thou, too, shalt rest...*

> *Тыншытарсың сен-даты*
> *Сабыр ұалсаң азырац...*

Dust sleeps on a road,
Leafage does not shake.
Wait a little more,
You'll too have a break.

"What a quiet, soothing feeling of night after the hot day blows in this little play by Goethe, translated so gracefully by our poet", - the much admired Belinsky.

Here, possibly, it would be appropriate to make a small digression and give (just for the sake of curiosity) three more translations of Goethe's miniature, which can serve as real reasons for comparative linguistic interpretation.

Translation by Bryusov V.:

Peace on all the tops
In the leafage, in valleys
None
Of the lines shall shake;
Birds are silent in the forest.
Just you wait: soon
You will fall asleep, too.

(interlinear translation)
Translation by Annensky I:

Over the mountain peaks the Silence sleeps.
In the leaves, already black,
You shan't feel a whiff.
In the thicket the flight is silent.
Oh, wait – a moment _
And the quietness will take... you.

(interlinear translation)
Translation by Alexandrov Y.:

Peace on the mountain peaks.
The rustle of leaves can hardly be heard.
In the wilderness of the forest
No singing and no fuss...

And you yourself in this shadow
Are closer and closer to repose.

(interlinear translation)

I think, the first "involuntary" conclusion from this comparative reading is best and its translation discloses an uncomfortable relationship: doesn't it? Indeed, a highly significant remark by L. N. Tolstoy comes to mind: "Of course, translation is nothing more than the reverse side of the carpet" - a paraphrase of Cervantes' Don Quixote, wherein it says: "... it is the same as a Flemish carpet from the inside".

Yet, we shall entrust the comparison of these translations to curious readers and focus more thoroughly on Lermontov's translation.

Herein is perfect precision. A literal match. Something noticeable even without detailed linguistic analysis. Lermontov took from Goethe "only" his theme, his idea. and expressed it in his own way. In this way he transposed the spirit of Goethe's poem into his own. This was Lermontov's key.

Here, since we are talking about the theme of Goethe's miniatures, it is worth, perhaps, to remind the reader there is a belief that the theme of "Wanderer's Night Song" was set by Ancient Greek poet Alcman (7th century BC). Y. Golosovker compiler and commentator of the book "The lyrics of Ancient Greece" (ACADEMIA 1935, M.-L.), emphasizes the evolution of the theme: Alcman - Goethe - Lermontov and discloses in the notes to the collection (p. 186) melos Alcman in translation of Veresaev:

Tops of high mountains and depths of dips sleep,
Cliffs and gorges sleep,
Snakes, how many of them
The black ground feeds,
Dense swarms of bees, animals of the high mountains,
And monsters in the crimson depth of the sea.
And the tribe
Of fast-flying birds sleeps, too.

(interlinear translation)

Doesn't this tell us the same thing – about the affinity of poetic muses?

However, we should not deviate from the main theme of our essay

Thus, the closeness of the set theme in Goethe and Lermontov is more obvious, concrete and convincing than in Alcman, although in lexical relation between the Goethe original and the translation of Lermontov are quite significant.

Lermontov brought not only, for example, separate definitions for individual words, but also completely "new" words, images, turns, completely absent in the original. He translated not the words, but style, tone, music of the poem. "Mountain peaks" sound like a Russian native poem, and not as something translated, alien. Perhaps that is why Lermontov did not translate its name "Wandrer's Nachtlied", but simply called the poem "From Goethe". Under this title, the poem first appeared in 1840 in the no.7 of "Notes of the Fatherland."

In the sense of absolute accuracy only the seventh and eighth verses coincide ("Warte nur, balde ruhest du auch" - "Want a little more – you, too, have a break"), the first and second verses are more or less close. As for the third, fourth, fifth and sixth verses, in Goethe they sound different.

In the two first lines Goethe emphasizes the exceptional silence ("O'er all the hilltops is quiet now"). Lermontov recreated it in fifth and sixth lines.

In order to do it, he introduces new details:

> Dust sleeps on a road,
> Leafage does not shake.

Speaking about the general silence, Goethe further details: "The birds are asleep in the trees". But in spite of the general peace, in Goethe's work all is "still in the tree-tops Hearest thou hardly a breath". Lermontov's translation describes absolute silence: Dust sleeps on a road, Leafage does not shake. If the poem was not called the "Night Song", the picture in the poem could describe, for instance, early morning. Yet, Lermontov is concrete. Concreteness is generally inherent to nature in the Russian language. This translation by Lermontov cannot be called

"Morning", "Summer Morning", "Early morning" or something else like that. He portrayed the night, specifically - the night only - night. The silence in his poem is the night silence and not silence in general, and tops of dreaming highlands "darken in the night". Goethe's tops are just tops in general, Lermontov's tops are the tops of highlands, which is specific, again. Lermontov expands this picture of the night, as if pushing its horizons, introduces quiet valleys (a purely Russian image), emphasizes night landscape with details like "fresh haze", "dark night".

Inspired to some extent by the abstract and philosophical worldview, of Goethe's poem in Lermontov's translation, one notices concretized, animated with visual details, colour painting. Thus, the picture of the night in "Mountain tops" becomes a kind of tangible, palpable, visible presence.

* * *

The muse of Pushkin and Lermontov was particularly close and clear to Abai.

"Pushkin and Lermontov ... both of them left the steppes, where their grandfathers lived, and ended their lives in the unknown expanses. But, during long winters, each became close to Abai. They appeared from another world, spoke different languages – yet they were treated warmly, like family. His twins in sorrow and sadness, they, having unraveled his soul told him, "And you with your thoughts are akin to us!"

These lines are from the epic of Mukhtar Auezov "Abai's Path".

There is a universal motif in these words. A motive ordered by consonance. A consonance of spirit. A unity in language diversity.

Certainly, in the 90s of the last century, Abai enthusiastically translated Lermontov's. "Confessions," "Hebrew Melody", "Do not Believe Yourself", "Alone I go out on the road", "Dagger", "Cliff", "Thought", "Bored and Sad", "Prayer", "Gifts of the Terek" and other works of the great Russian poet, Also, Abai brilliantly translated the originality in Lermontov's muse.

During those years he translated "Mountain Peaks".

This is Abai's mature translation:

> Қараңғы түнде тау қалғып,
> Ұйқыға кетер балбырап.
> Даланы жым-жырт дел-сал қып,
> Түн басады салбырып.
>
> Шаң шығармас жол дағы,
> Сыбдырламас жапырақ.
> Тыншығарсың сен дағы
> Сабыр қылсаң азырақ.

How subtly and emotionally great poets understood each other!

After all, Abai's translation is amazingly close to Lermontov's text, while the differences are suggestive.

For the Russian reader, I shall give the reverse interlinear translation:

> *In the dark night mountains, napping,*
> *Go to sleep, having lounged.*
> *The night hangs over*
> *The drowsy quiet steppe,*
> *The road shows no dust,*
> *The leaves do not rustle (whisper).*
> *And you shall rest too,*
> *If you show some composure.*
>
> *(interlinear translation)*

Since childhood, I, like every Kazakh, remembered these verses by heart. Having written them down as they were sung in the aul where I grew up, I, just in case, took a look in one of Abai's last collections and wondered: instead of «сыбдырламас жапырақ» there is «сілкіне алмас жапырақ,», i.e. "leaves do not rustle" — "leaves do not quiver". There is no principal difference, and so I left the line as I had known it since childhood. Alas, textual "Abai Studies" are far from exemplary and there is still no canonical edition of his works.

So, speaking of Abai's translation.

In Lermontov's version there's already night, late night, while in Abai's the night only dusks: the mountains, napping, are only falling asleep, while night falls, hanging over the steppe. In the first quatrain by

Lermontov there's only one verb ("tops of dreaming highlands darken in the night"), yet Abai, additionally has the verb "leave" (*«кетер»*), "falls" (*«түн басады»*), - also there are gerunds "having lounged" (*«балбырап»*), "napping" (*«қалғып»*), and *«дел-сал қып»* **which** is actually a verbal form. Using such an abundance of verbs and verbal forms, Abai showed the movement of the night. Its smooth, wide, majestic step - its peace and silence. Undoubtedly, this is what the reader feels in the poem by Abai. We do not only see the night, as in Goethe and Lermontov, but equally we feel the coming of this night. In a sense, it is a frozen, static picture of night expanded, dare I suggest, with a vibrancy even more dynamic than Lermontov.

In the above quotation from Belinsky, we read of a "quiet, soothing feeling of the night after a hot day." However, none of Goethe;s lines, or transcriptions by Lermontov, evocatively paint the night in this manner -

For his part, Abai was acquainted with the article of Belinsky "Poemsby M. Lermontov" and, obviously, the translation of "Mountain peaks" was made after he read it. When working with it, however, Abai uses words like "having lounged", "napping", "exhausted-prostrated" to give the feeling of night imediately after a hot day.

Furthermore, one can note Lermontov's "valleys" replaced by the "steppe" - quite consciously, of course (valley in Kazakh is *аңғар, алап, алқап*). If Abai instead of *«даланы»* would have written *«аңғарды»*, *«алапты»* or *«алқапты»*, the rhythm would not have changed. All these words are two-syllables in the original form, but they would not be as relevant. Although, a lesser poet probably would have done it, trying to be closer to the text. Here, for the sake of interest, I give (for those who know Kazakh language) the translation of "Mountain Tops" by Muszaphar Alibayev:

> *Мақпалдай қара түндерде*
> *Маужырап таулар мүлгіді.*
> *Тым-тырыс, бей-жай қыр-белде*
> *Қоңыржай мұнар сырғиды.*
> *Бұрқ етпес шаң да жолдағы,*
> *Желпінбес жасыл шалғын да.*
> *Аялдай тұрсаң болғаны,*

Тыныстар күниң алдыңда.

When translating, therefore, M. Alimbaev also followed the translation of Lermontov and not the original.

Nonetheless, it was Abai who best comprehended the image. Describing the night of Lermontov, he saw and felt the poetry of a "Kazakh night - the night of the Kazakh steppe".

Once translated by Abai "Mountain Peaks" sounded marvelous in Kazakh, while at same time, it kept the thread of spiritual intimacy with Goethe's original.

* * *

Such a spiritual connection between all great poets exists and manifests everywhere. I felt this one day when walking through the quiet, thoughtful halls of the State Museum of Literature named after Alisher Navoi in Tashkent. Holding my breath, I examined ancient books and manuscripts. There were many of them, large and small, graceful and bulky, darkened by time, by the dust of centuries, but preserved.

The quantity of labour and love showered by scribes on these priceless manuscripts, books of poetry and divans, astounded me! The quaint oriental ornaments made with cold embossing was delightful. Exquisite pictures, densely arranged around four to six lines on a page covered with gold specks, truly inspiring, As was the thin, interlacing lines, delicate ligature and diligence portrayed in the liquid pure gold within. Amazingly, their beauty seemed imperishable. They had neither faded, nor frayed. One can understand Goethe's passion, I suspect, when examining the poetry of the East copied and lovingly marked with magic signs. As if immersing myself in the old days, I reverently whispered the sweet names: Navoi, Hafiz, Saadi, Ferdowsi, Nizami, Jami, Fizuli. And recalled: once young Abai had returned from Semipalatinsk madrasah, whispering, like a healing prayer, these very same names in the ear of his beloved grandmother Zera. At that moment, I was glad to see Abai in one of the halls among the great poets of the East.

Slightly before this, Goethe (having come into contact with the seven celebrated "kings of the poets"), uttered – with his German accent on the first syllable - these wonderful names to himself. To verify this, readers are invited to look through his "West-Eastern Divan" to see their presence. Indeed, in his youthful poetry, Abai equally recited these glorious names - Fizuli, Saihan, Navoi, Saadi, Ferdowsi, Hafiz.

Yes... the East with its poetry, philosophy, colorful everyday life and vibrant sensuality, has always attracted the West, whilst the best minds of the West have always sought rapprochement with eastern cultures. Thus, we may read about the same Divinity of East and West:

> *God created the East,*
> *The West was his creation, too.*

Many decades later the same idea was expressed by our contemporary Olzhas Suleimenov:

> *There is no East,*
> *And there is no West,*
> *There is no end of the heavens.*
> *No East,*
> *And no West —*
> *Father has two sons.*
> *No East,*
> *And no West,*
> *There are*
> *Sunrise and sunset,*
> *There is a big word —*
> *THE EARTH.*
>
> *(interlinear translation)*

Unmistakably, those who share Poetry have discovered a mutual divine mystery, a divine miracle.

* * *

As such, Abai not only translated" Wanderer's Night Song" into the Kazakh language, and composed music suitable for a Kazakh who would not know this wise, melodic song «In the dark night mountains, napping ... « and so on.

In 1958, in the Zhambyl region, in Baikadam, where I was a teacher, I once told E. I. Schüller (an old colleague) about this project. A conversation energizing him to start singing in a booming deep bass: "Ober alien Gipfeln .." I still don't know who owns the music written to the words of Goethe. Perhaps, the composer Zelter, friend of the poet? Anyway, I was struck by the fact that the beginning of this music is surprisingly similar to Abai's melody. The same tone, the same slow, gradually, increasing, lyricism. From where did such harmony come from? Maybe it is the mysterious affinity betwixt muses again?

I don't know…

But one thing is clear – there is something magical in this universal melody of Abai's. The reason, possibly, is that it is sung by Kazakhs when they find themselves in a circle of friendship with Europeans. Is it also because they feel in Abai's song something pf kinship?

Here Abdizhamil Nurpeisov recalls: «It was in Paris on the eve of the Christmas holidays - after some concert of youth - I was taken to the house of a lean, bearded composer. A lot of people had gathered there, and after a light treat, we began to sing - and sang with pleasure for a long time. The atmosphere was wonderfully warm and friendly, the mood was elated, and I, reserved by nature, suddenly felt a pleasant ease. Thus, I also sang, being caught up as best as I could, venturing to sing a song of Abai "Mountains in the dark night, napping…", composed to the poem by Goethe into our Kazakh language. "Is it really composed by a Kazakh? — One of guests was surprised. – As the tune sounds European…" I smiled, having recalled the amazing, truly unique event that befell the famous poem …"[49]

* * *

Consonance… It is everywhere.

In nature. In music. In poetry. In lofty and noble impulses of the passions. In human hearts. In human speech.

The poet said:

[49]   "Consonance ", Alma-Ata," Zhalyn ", 1982, p. 5

There is a graceful power
In consonance of lively words

(Lermontov)

There is consonance of the spirit. Consonance of talent. A unity of language diversity.

Here, for example, are Goethe and Abai. A careful, soul-sighted reader cannot fail to be excited by a certain proximity between these two giants of the human spirit. As such, one cannot help but imagine some kind of relationship, a kind of consonance worthy of discussion. Grasp the meaning behind the poetry of Goethe and Abai, then read the great maxims of the gakliya by the great steppe dweller - how many echoes of thoughts and feelings arise! German and Kazakh, their roles are complimentary. Uncannily, each poet perfectly knew his worth. Thus, Goethe wrote in his diary: "Unfortunately, I feel my thirty years and my global significance!" Later life and deeds demonstrated that he was entitled to such recognition. So recalled, Abai makes mention of his renown in one poem: "Dzhigits, my gist is not simple". He was not exaggerating either when speaking of his mystery.

Together, they, Goethe and Abai, were the spokesmen of their era. They embody the spirit of their Time. All, I think, explaining their kinship.

* * *

The appeal and charm of Abai's version of "Mountains in the dark night, napping..." is enormous. Nowadays, it is sung everywhere, alone and in a choir, at a feast, or on the stage: always exciting as well as mesmerizing his descendants. Sometimes in the most unexpected of ways.

In 1970, writers from the GDR were visiting Alma-Ata. One sunny day, Kazakh colleagues drove them to the mountains, and there, in the deep cool shade of the Tien-Shan fir trees the famous Kazakh poet Tursynhan Abdrakhmanova suddenly started singing in her beautiful voice «Қараңғы түнде тау қалғып...» Shocked, these guests from the GDR, (particularly writer Ruth Kraft) thought Tursynhan was singing her own poems, but afterwards learned what she sang, They were delighted. "How? Goethe?! Here in Kazakhstan, in the Alatau mountains!" - she exclaimed. It seemed to her in that moment, amid the green and lush hills of Thuringia, something magical had occurred.

Thereafter, Ruth Kraft wrote a lyrical essay entitled "Friends at Alatau" and published it in the "Neue Deutsche Literature" (1970, no. 8).

There are many such coincidences. They are listed here, along with facts, some of my own observations and experiences and the potential motivation behind my short story and its fictional hero, Captain Erzhanov. Digressing slightly, allow me to explain that in the first year after the war (at the behest of my fantasy) he takes a walk to Kikelhan to fulfill his youthful dream - to worship at places known to Goethe. Indeed, I vividly imagine him as a young Kazakh philologist who, after four years of conflict, had happily preserved his enthusiastic ardour. As he stands, therefore, alone on a green ridge, he begins to sing:

Mountains in the dark night, napping
Fall asleep, having lounged...

He is glad to be alive, young and full of energy. All making him realize, probably for the first time, these words and music also belong to Abai. It seems that the ravishing night of the Kazakh steppe equally falls on the slopes of German mountains. Exactly like, those people of the infinite expanses of the Morgenland - Morning country. On this night, having easily surmounted unfathomable space, Abai's dark-complexioned Muse flew on a date with the spirit of Goethe, while Erzhanov feels the only witness of this event.

Unarguably, this song of Goethe's wanderer - having absorbed the feather-wormwood flavour of the free steppes (dressed in their stately plangent sounds), becomes omnipresent across both

East and West.

Experiencing an almost inexplicable pride in Arbay's achievements, Erzhanov senses he sang for the first time in his life with sublime feelings. "Peace to you, Goethe", he exhales. Peace to you, great poet of Kazakhstan!"

Back then, when I was writing this story, I had no idea I had invented such a character. Yet life, as was long ago observed, is richer than fiction. Hence, a real prototype of my Yerzhanov charcter lived literally next door to me. At a distance of one trolley stop, Moreover, I had been meeting with him over the years almost every day. In reality, his name is Kalmuhan Isabaev - my oldest friend and fellow writer.

At this juncture, I have to tell readers how the neighborhood of Ilmenau, fantastically and happily entwined with the fate of the Kazakh writer Kalmuhan Isabaev.

It so happened that, in 1949-55, a young Soviet officer named Kalmuhan Isabaev became a friend of the builders of the new German democracy: a colleague of those who were called "activists of the first hour" in the GDR. Here, he found inspiration in the immortal genius of Goethe. As such, Kalmuhan often walked around the neighborhood: a quiet, cozy town fill of history. Indeed, he admired the local hunting lodge and sketched it. Kalmuhan later recalling: "When I went upstairs in Goethe's hunting hut, a part of Thuringia stretched out in front of me and I could not resist it – So, I sang the song of Abai, which in a far corner of the earth, he had immortalized on behalf of Goethe."

Perhaps, it was that blessed land, as well as this people's thrifty memory of the Poet, which awoke the young Kazakh officer's gift as a writer? Anyway, whatever it was, stories, characters, and ideas for future works were born through his impressions of Ilmenau.

Having demobilized, and having arrived in Alma-Ata, Kalmuhan Isabaev then plunged into everyday worries. Although, simultaneously, he studied, worked, wrote stories and novels. All the time remembering his well-loved faraway place in the small district of Suhl. He additionally remembered his loyal friends and most of all – a path through green hills to the hunting lodge where Goethe used to go in his youth. Also, he recalled with excitement how he climbed to the top of the hill as a young officer anxiously imagining his distant homeland - colorful Bayanaul. It was then his dream of returning to this location exciting him and his work on Abai was born

This dream came true - in July, 1979.

Receiving an invitation from the Union of Writers of the GDR, Isabaev immediately decided he would go to the Suhl district. Indeed, he would walk to the top of Gabelbah and take with him a gift for the local Goethe museum - a marble slab with a stamped text of "Wanderer's Night Song" (as translated by Abai) and a tape recording of the song by the famous singer Magav'ya Koshkinbaev - to his own accompaniment on the dombra. Thence, after meeting with German friends following a twenty-five year separation, the excited Kazakh writer made further plans. Certainly, everything in that land was both familiar and new to him, while the true apogee of his meeting was a solemn gathering (organized for July 22, 1979) at the hall of the Goethe Museum in Gabelbah. Thusly, in the presence of the party leadership, famous scientists and members of the public, a concert was held - in the museum wherein a memorial plaque with the text of Abai's «Wanderer's Night Song « was installed.

Above the text on a silhouette of Alatau was the inscription: «Goethe. *Wandrers Nachtlied*. 1780. - Lermontov. Mountain peaks. 1840.- Abai. Тұнп Тау. 1892" The participants listened to the enchanting melody of Abai with interest - catching the consonant mood of Goethe's night wanderer.

Now 60-70 thousand people - that is the average attendance of the Goethe museum in Gabelbahe per year – leave this ancient abode, whilst listening to «mountains in the dark night, napping.". Back then, it was also noted this was the first time Goethe's creation (translated into a Turkic language), had returned to its birthplace. As such, the first secretary of the SED district committee of Ilmenau (comrade Heinz Koch) gave a banquet in honor of Abai. A banquet in the same hall to which Goethe made a special trip from Weimar on August 26, 1831, and celebrated his last birthday.

Happy and rejuvenated Kalmuhan returned from the GDR. Moreover, this ceremonial act of placing a memorial plaque in the Goethe Museum received widespread media coverage in both the GDR and the Soviet Union. The author himself eulogizing his trip. Immediately, letters and enthusiastic messages were received by the writer! Less than a year later, in May 1980 (on the occasion of the 35th anniversary of the liberation of the German people from Hitler's fascism), Kalmuhan was invited back to the GDR. Again, he was the guest of honour of the Suhl Region, and again he visited his blessed land - "the green heart of Thuringia". Obviously, the writer didn't go to Goethe Museum empty-handed. Proudly, he brought a portrait of Abai (made by him), along with a musical notation of the tune «mountains in the dark night, napping.." and a dombra - with inscriptions in Russian and German under unbreakable glass. It read,

"Asia's first translator of Goethe – the poet and composer Abai on a traditional musical instrument."

On May 6, 1980 the writer handed this gift to the Kulturbund district offices - whilst the next day the newspaper "Freies Wort" reported it. This remarkable case lead countrymen of Abai to the idea of erecting a monument to this immortal song. So, in the summer of 1983 "at the request of the population," - as it was noted by the local press - a monument was raised in the center of the Semipalatinsk region of Kazakhstan – in Karaul city. On the bas-relief portraits of the great poets - Goethe, Lermontov, and Abai were depicted, along with the full text of "Wandrers Nachtlied" in German, Russian and the Kazakh language. The place is now called "Alley of poets."

When celebrating the 40th anniversary of Liberation Day, the party leadership of Suhl County invited Kalmuhan to the GDR for a third event. This time, he was presented with the Goethe Museums tablet entitled "Kazakh interpreters of Goethe". The plate is informative: a portrait of Abai by Kalmuhan (from the Murseit manuscript), tops it saying,

A musical notation of "Wanderer's Night Song", photocopy of the decision of the Executive Committee of the City Council of the People's Deputies of Semipalatinsk to rename the Civil street - in the street named after Johann Wolfgang von Goethe, Goethe's "Selected poetry" cover photo in the Kazakh language, picture of bas-relief Karaul city, photocopy of the page "Faust" in the Kazakh edition, portraits of the main interpreters of Goethe in the Kazakh language – Bekhozhin K., Shangitbaev K., Imanasov S., Kurmanov M., Egeubaev A. listing the names of translated poems of Goethe in German and Kazakh languages.

Thanks to the enthusiasm and tireless efforts of K. Isabaev streets in the cities of Semipalatinsk , Tselinograd and Abai were named after Goethe.

Everything told by me is just one part of an extensive history of cultural relations between peoples, a small but remarkable fact, which has found an echo in hearts of good people. A fact that characterizes the spirit of consonance. The unity of language diversity.

... The wonderful chant of Abai float over the night aul. As if somewhere from that height one can hear the smoothly and calmly floating singer's voice.

Wait; soon like these
Thou, too, shalt rest…

    The fate of Goethe's wanderer turned out to be happy. His night song was heard and caught up by the great poets, Lermontov and Abai, and lovingly brought to their peoples. And now, through ages and distances, it floats over the steppe, over the valleys and ridges of the mountains, glorifying peace and silence, promising all strangers in the land a coveted peace.

1970—1986

Belger Herold

Goethe and Abai: Essay.— Almaty: Zhalyn, 1989—104p.

Well-known Kazakh prose writer, critic and translator Herold Belger for many years enthusiastically worked on the theme of "Goethe and Abai". In the work of two national geniuses of the German and Kazakh peoples the researcher finds many themes and motifs of their spiritual harmony, apparent affinity of the Muses. A clear entanglement in their destiny, searches and impulses.

HERTFORDSHIRE PRESS

Title List

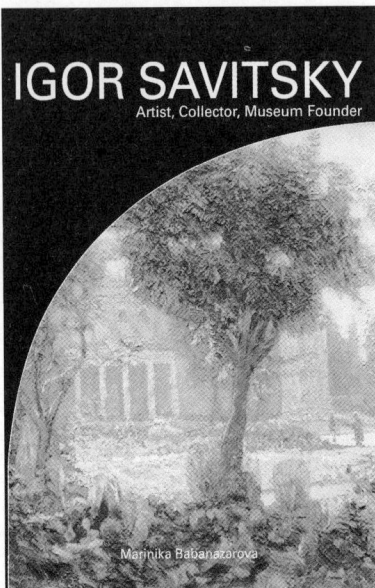

Igor Savitsky: Artist, Collector, Museum Founder
by Marinika Babanazarova (2011)

Since the early 2000s, Igor Savitsky's life and accomplishments have earned increasing international recognition. He and the museum he founded in Nukus, the capital of Karakalpakstan in the far northwest of Uzbekistan. Marinika Babanazarova's memoir is based on her 1990 graduate dissertation at the Tashkent Theatre and Art Institute. It draws upon correspondence, official records, and other documents about the Savitsky family that have become available during the last few years, as well as the recollections of a wide range of people who knew Igor Savitsky personally.

Игорь Савитский: художник, собиратель, основатель музея

С начала 2000-х годов, жизнь и достижения Игоря Савицкого получили широкое признание во всем мире. Он и его музей, основанный в Нукусе, столице Каракалпакстана, стали предметом многочисленных статей в мировых газетах и журналах, таких как TheGuardian и NewYorkTimes, телевизионных программ в Австралии, Германии и Японии. Книга издана на русском, английском и французском языках.

Igor Savitski: Peintre, collectionneur, fondateur du Musée (French), (2012)

Le mémoire de Mme Babanazarova, basé sur sa thèse de 1990 à l'Institut de Théâtre et D'art de Tachkent, s'appuie sur la correspondance, les dossiers officiels et d'autres documents d'Igor Savitsky et de sa famille, qui sont devenus disponibles dernièrement, ainsi que sur les souvenirs de nombreuses personnes ayant connu Savistky personellement, ainsi que sur sa propre expérience de travail a ses cotés, en tant que successeur designé. son nom a titre posthume.

LANGUAGE: **ENG, RUS, FR**   ISBN: **978-0955754999**   RRP: **£10.00**
AVAILABLE ON **KINDLE**

Savitsky Collection Selected Masterpieces.
Poster set of 8 posters (2014)

Limited edition of prints from the world-renowned Museum of Igor Savitsky in Nukus, Uzbekistan. The set includs nine of the most famous works from the Savitsky collection wrapped in a colourful envelope. Selected Masterpieces of the Savitsky Collection.

[Cover] BullVasily Lysenko 1. Oriental Café Aleksei Isupov 2. Rendezvous Sergei Luppov 3. By the Sea. Marie-LouiseKliment Red'ko 4. Apocalypse Aleksei Rybnikov 5. Rain Irina Shtange 6. Purple Autumn Ural Tansykbayaev 7. To the Train Viktor Ufimtsev 8. Brigade to the fields Alexander Volkov This museum, also known as the Nukus Museum or the Savitsky

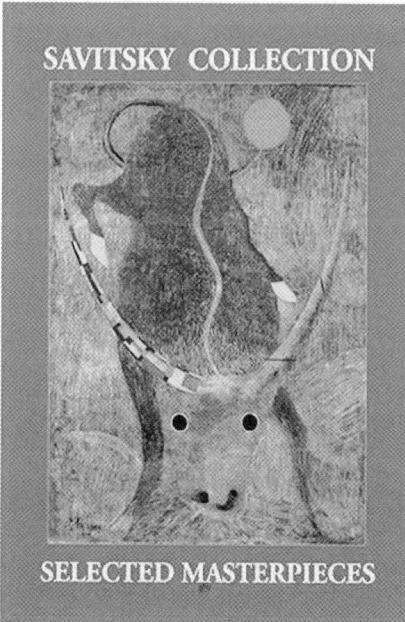

ISBN: **9780992787387**
RRP: **£25.00**

Friendly Steppes. A Silk Road Journey
by Nick Rowan

This is the chronicle of an extraordinary adventure that led Nick Rowan to some of the world's most incredible and hidden places. Intertwined with the magic of 2,000 years of Silk Road history, he recounts his experiences coupled with a remarkable realisation of just what an impact this trade route has had on our society as we know it today. Containing colourful stories, beautiful photography and vivid characters, and wrapped in the local myths and legends told by the people Nick met and who live along the route, this is both a travelogue and an education of a part of the world that has remained hidden for hundreds of years.

HARD BACK ISBN: **978-0-9927873-4-9**
PAPERBACK ISBN: **978-0-9557549-4-4**
RRP: **£14.95**
AVAILABLE ON **KINDLE**

Birds of Uzbeksitan
by Nedosekov (2012)

FIRST AND ONLY PHOTOALBUM
OF UZBEKISTAN BIRDS!

This book, which provides an introduction to the birdlife of Uzbekistan, is a welcome addition to the tools available to those working to conserve the natural heritage of the country. In addition to being the first photographic guide to the birds of Uzbekistan, the book is unique in only using photographs taken within the country. The compilers are to be congratulated on preparing an attractive and accessible work which hopefully will encourage more people to discover the rich birdlife of the country and want to protect it for future generations

HARD BACK
ISBN: **978-0-955754913**
RRP: **£25.00**

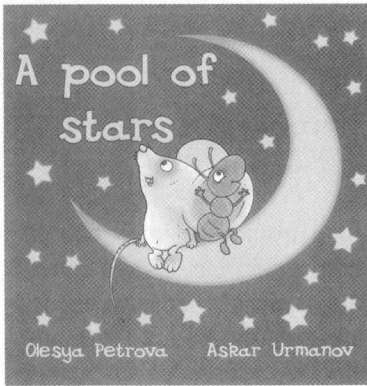

Pool of Stars
by Olesya Petrova, Askar Urmanov,
English Edition (2007)

It is the first publication of a young writer Olesya Petrova, a talented and creative person. Fairy-tale characters dwell on this book's pages. Lovely illustrations make this book even more interesting to kids, thanks to a remarkable artist Askar Urmanov. We hope that our young readers will be very happy with such a gift. It's a book that everyone will appreciate. For the young, innocent ones - it's a good source of lessons they'll need in life. For the not-so-young but young at heart, it's a great book to remind us that life is so much more than work.

ISBN: **978-0955754906 ENGLISH** AVAILABLE ON **KINDLE**

«Звёздная лужица»

Первая книга для детей, изданная британским издательством Hertfordshire Press. Это также первая публикация молодой талантливой писательницы Олеси Петровой. Сказочные персонажи живут на страницах этой книги. Прекрасные иллюстрации делают книгу еще более интересной и красочной для детей, благодаря замечательному художнику Аскару Урманову. Вместе Аскар и Олеся составляют удивительный творческий тандем, который привнес жизнь в эту маленькую книгу

ISBN: **978-0955754906 RUSSIAN**
RRP: **£4.95**

Buyuk Temurhon (Tamerlane)
by C. Marlowe, Uzbek Edition (2010)

Hertfordshire based publisher Silk Road Media, run by Marat Akhmedjanov, and the BBC Uzbek Service have published one of Christopher Marlowe's famous plays, Tamburlaine the Great, translated into the Uzbek language. It is the first of Christopher Marlowe's plays to be translated into Uzbek, which is Tamburlaine's native language. Translated by Hamid Ismailov, the current BBC World Service Writer-in-Residence, this new publication seeks to introduce English classics to Uzbek readers worldwide.

PAPERBACK
ISBN: **9780955754982**
RRP: **£10.00**
AVAILABLE ON **KINDLE**

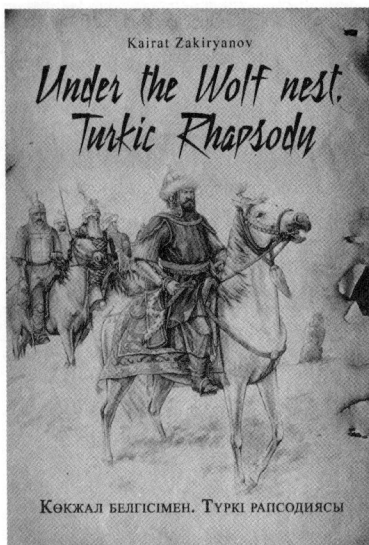

Under Wolf's Nest
by KairatZakiryanov
English –Kazakh edition

Were the origins of Islam, Christianity and the legend of King Arthur all influenced by steppe nomads from Kazakhstan? Ranging through thousands of years of history, and drawing on sources from Herodotus through to contemporary Kazakh and Russian research, the crucial role in the creation of modern civilisation played by the Turkic people is revealed in this detailed yet highly accessible work. Professor Kairat Zakiryanov, President of the Kazakh Academy of Sport and Tourism, explains how generations of steppe nomads, including Genghis Khan, have helped shape the language, culture and populations of Asia, Europe, the Middle East and America through migrations taking place over millennia.

HARD BACK
ISBN: **9780957480728**
RRP: **£17.50**
AVAILABLE ON **KINDLE**

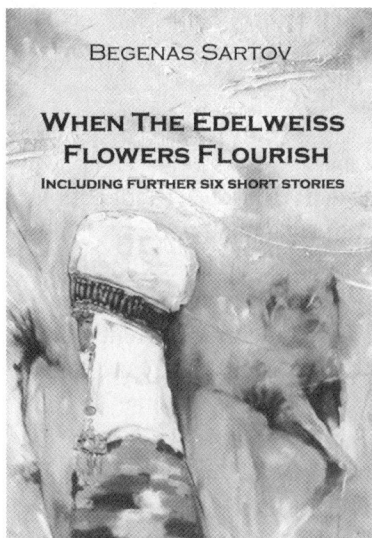

When Edelweiss flowers flourish
by Begenas Saratov
English edition (2012)

A spectacular insight into life in the Soviet Union in the late 1960's made all the more intriguing by its setting within the Sovet Republic of Kyrgyzstan. The story explores Soviet life, traditional Kyrgyz life and life on planet Earth through a Science Fiction story based around an alien nations plundering of the planet for life giving herbs. The author reveals far sighted thoughts and concerns for conservation, management of natural resources and dialogue to achieve peace yet at the same time shows extraordinary foresight with ideas for future technologies and the progress of science. The whole style of the writing gives a fascinating insight into the many facets of life in a highly civilised yet rarely known part of the world.

ISBN: **978-0955754951**   **PAPERBACK**   AVAILABLE ON **KINDLE**

Mamyry gyldogon maalda

Это фантастический рассказ, повествующий о советской жизни, жизни кыргызского народа и о жизни на планете в целом. Автор рассказывает об инопланетных народах, которые пришли на нашу планету, чтобы разграбить ее. Автор раскрывает дальновидность мысли о сохранение и рациональном использовании природных ресурсов, а также диалога для достижения мира и в то же время показывает необычайную дальновидность с идеями для будущих технологий и прогресса науки. Книга также издана на **кыргызском языке**.

ISBN: **9780955754951**
RRP: **£12.95**

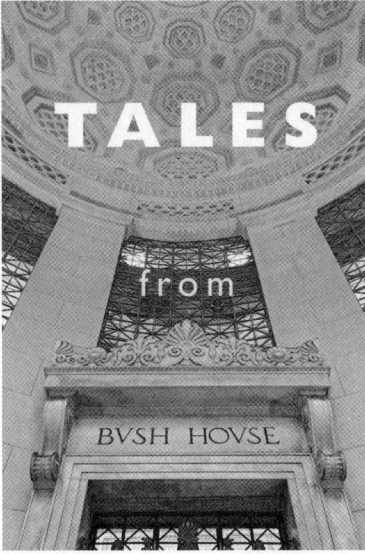

Tales from Bush House
(BBC Wolrd Service)
by Hamid Ismailov
(2012)

Tales From Bush House is a collection of short narratives about working lives, mostly real and comic, sometimes poignant or apocryphal, gifted to the editors by former and current BBC World Service employees. They are tales from inside Bush House - the home of the World Service since 1941 - escaping through its marble-clad walls at a time when its staff begin their departure to new premises in Portland Place. In July 2012, the grand doors of this imposing building will close on a vibrant chapter in the history of Britain's most cosmopolitan organisation. So this is a timely book.

PAPERBACK
ISBN: **9780955754975**
RRP: **£12.95**
AVAILABLE ON **KINDLE**

Chants of Dark Fire
(Песни темного огня)
by Zhulduz Baizakova
Russian edition (2012)

This contemporary work of poetry contains the deep and inspirational rhythms of the ancient Steppe. It combines the nomad, modern, postmodern influences in Kazakhstani culture in the early 21st century, and reveals the hidden depths of contrasts, darkness, and longing for light that breathes both ice and fire to inspire a rich form of poetry worthy of reading and contemplating. It is also distinguished by the uniqueness of its style and substance. Simply sublime, it has to be read and felt for real.

ISBN: **978-0957480711**
RRP: **£10.00**

Kamila
by R. Karimov
Kyrgyz – Uzbek Edition (2013)

«Камила» - это история о сироте, растущей на юге Кыргызстана. Наряду с личной трагедией Камилы и ее родителей, Рахим Каримов описывает очень реалистично и подробно местный образ жизни. Роман выиграл конкурс "Искусство книги-2005" в Бишкеке и был признан национальным бестселлером Книжной палаты Кыргызской Республики.

PAPERBACK
ISBN: **978-0957480773**
RRP: **£10.00**

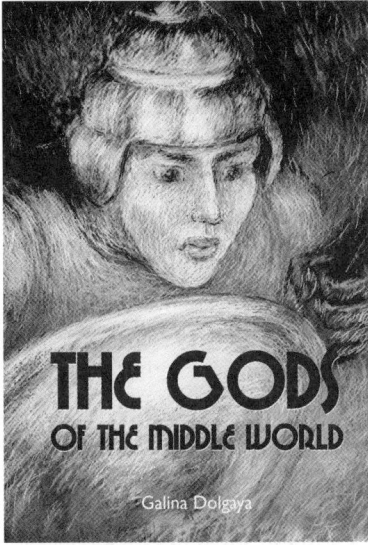

THE GODS
OF THE MIDDLE WORLD

Galina Dolgaya

Gods of the Middle World
by Galina Dolgaya (2013)

The Gods of the Middle World tells the story of Sima, a student of archaeology for whom the old lore and ways of the Central Asian steppe peoples are as vivid as the present. When she joints a group of archaeologists in southern Kazakhstan, asking all the time whether it is really possible to 'commune with the spirits', she soon discovers the answer first hand, setting in motion events in the spirit world that have been frozen for centuries. Meanwhile three millennia earlier, on the same spot, a young woman and her companion struggle to survive and amend wrongs that have caused the neighbouring tribe to take revenge. The two narratives mirror one another, and Sima's destiny is to resolve the ancient wrongs in her own lifetime and so restore the proper balance of the forces of good and evil

PAPERBACK
ISBN: **978-0957480797**
RRP: **£14.95**
AVAILABLE ON **KINDLE**

Jazz Book, poetry
by Alma Sharipova , Russian Edition

Сборник стихов Алмы Шариповой
JazzCafé, в котором предлагаются
стихотворения, написанные в разное
время и посвященые различным
событиям из жизни автора.
Стихотворения Алмы содержательные
и эмоциональные одновременно,
отражают философию ее отношения
к происходящему. Почти каждое
стихотворение представляет
собой законченный рассказ
в миниатюре. Сюжет разворачивается
последовательно и завершается
небольшим резюме в последних
строках. Стихотворения раскрываются, как готовые «формулы»
жизни. Читатель невольно задумывается над ними и может найти как
что-то знакомое, так и новое для себя.

ISBN: 978-0-957480797
RRP: £10.00

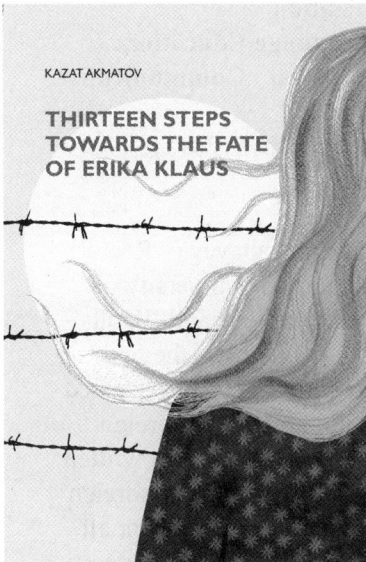

13 steps of Erika Klaus
by Kazat Akmatov (2013)

The story involves the harrowing experiences of a young and very naïve Norwegian woman who has come to Kyrgyzstan to teach English to schoolchildren in a remote mountain outpost. Governed by the megalomaniac Colonel Bronza, the community barely survives under a cruel and unjust neo-fascist regime. Immersed in the local culture, Erika is initially both enchanted and apprehensive but soon becomes disillusioned as day after day, she is forbidden to teach. Alongside Erika's story, are the personal tragedies experienced by former soldier Sovietbek , Stalbek, the local policeman, the Principal of the school and a young man who has married a Kyrgyz refugee from Afghanistan . Each tries in vain, to challenge and change the corrupt political situation in which they are forced to live.

PAPERBACK
ISBN: **978-0957480766**
RRP: **£12.95**
AVAILABLE ON **KINDLE**

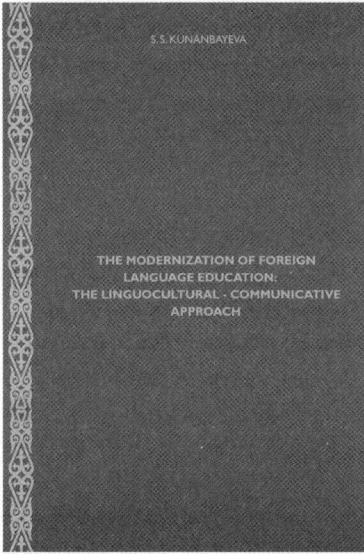

**The Modernization
of Foreign Language Education:
The Linguocultural - Communicative
Approach**
by SalimaKunanbayeva (2013)

Professor S. S. Kunanbayeva - Rector
of Ablai Khan Kazakh University
of International Relations and World
Languages This textbook is the first
of its kind in Kazakhstan to be devoted
to the theory and practice of foreign
language education. It has been written
primarily for future teachers of foreign
languages and in a wider sense for all
those who to be interested in the question
(in the problems?) of the study and use of foreign languages. This book
outlines an integrated theory of modern foreign language learning (FLL)
which has been drawn up and approved under the auspices of the school
of science and methodology of Kazakhstan's Ablai Khan University
of International Relations and World Languages.

PAPERBACK
ISBN: **978-0957480780**
RRP: **£19.95**
AVAILABLE ON **KINDLE**

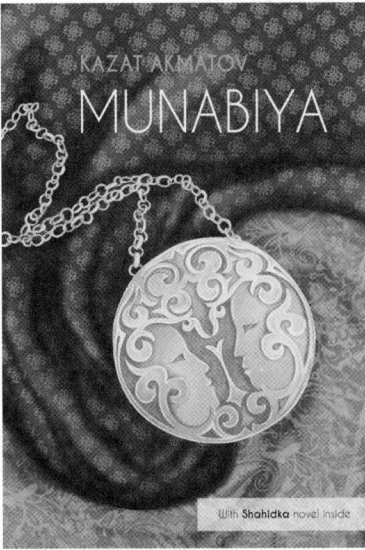

Shahidka/ Munabia
by KazatAkmatov (2013)

Munabiya and Shahidka by Kazat Akmatov National Writer of Kyrgyzstan Recently translated into English Akmatov's two love stories are set in rural Kyrgyzstan, where the natural environment, local culture, traditions and political climate all play an integral part in the dramas which unfold. Munabiya is a tale of a family's frustration, fury, sadness and eventual acceptance of a long term love affair between the widowed father and his mistress. In contrast, Shahidka is a multi-stranded story which focuses on the ties which bind a series of individuals to the tragic and ill-fated union between a local Russian girl and her Chechen lover, within a multi-cultural community where violence, corruption and propaganda are part of everyday life.

PAPERBACK
ISBN: **978-0957480759**
RRP: **£12.95**
AVAILABLE ON **KINDLE**

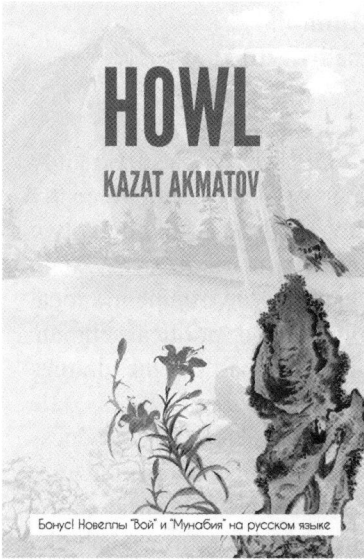

Howl *novel*
by Kazat Akmatov (2014)
English –Russian

The "Howl" by Kazat Akmatov is a beautifully crafted novel centred on life in rural Kyrgyzstan. Characteristic of the country's national writer, the simple plot is imbued with descriptions of the spectacular landscape, wildlife and local customs. The theme however, is universal and the contradictory emotions experienced by Kalen the shepherd must surely ring true to young men, and their parents, the world over. Here is a haunting and sensitively written story of a bitter -sweet rite of passage from boyhood to manhood.

PAPERBACK
ISBN: **978-0993044410**
RRP: **£12.50**
AVAILABLE ON **KINDLE**

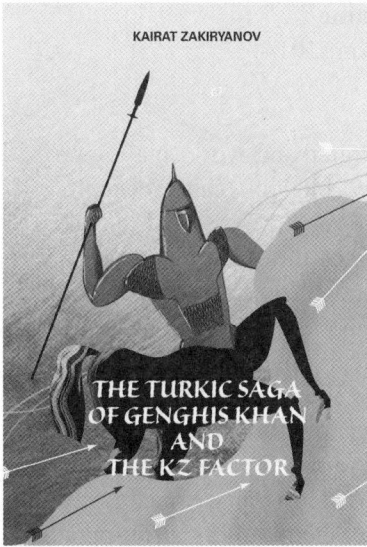

The Turkic Saga
of Genghis Khan and the KZ Factor
by Dr.Kairat Zakiryanov (2014)

An in-depth study of Genghis Khan from a Kazakh perspective, The Turkic Saga of Genghis Khan presupposes that the great Mongol leader and his tribal setting had more in common with the ancestors of the Kazakhs than with the people who today identify as Mongols. This idea is growing in currency in both western and eastern scholarship and is challenging both old Western assumptions and the long-obsolete Soviet perspective. This is an academic work that draws on many Central Asian and Russian sources and often has a Eurasianist bias - while also paying attention to new accounts by Western authors such as Jack Weatherford and John Man. It bears the mark of an independent, unorthodox and passionate scholar.

HARD BACK
ISBN: **978-0992787370**
RRP: **£17.50**
AVAILABLE ON **KINDLE**

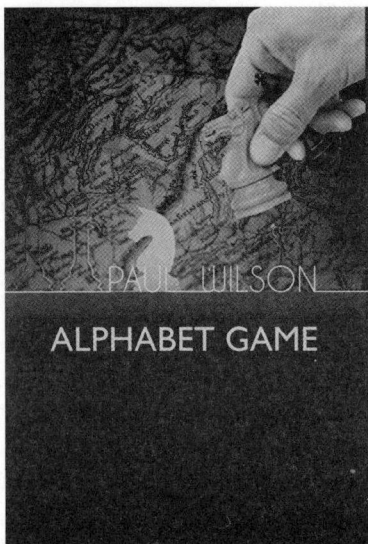

Alphabet Game
by Paul Wilson (2014)

Travelling around the world may appear as easy as ABC, but looks can be deceptive: there is no 'X' for a start. Not since Xidakistan was struck from the map. Yet post 9/11, with the War on Terror going global, could 'The Valley' be about to regain its place on the political stage? Xidakistan's fate is inextricably linked with that of Graham Ruff, founder of Ruff Guides. Setting sail where Around the World in Eighty Days and Lost Horizon weighed anchor, our not-quite-a-hero suffers all in pursuit of his golden triangle: The Game, The Guidebook, The Girl. With the future of printed Guidebooks increasingly in question, As Evelyn Waugh's Scoop did for Foreign Correspondents the world over, so this novel lifts the lid on Travel Writers for good.

PAPERBACK
ISBN: **978-0-992787325**
RRP: **£14.95**
AVAILABLE ON **KINDLE**

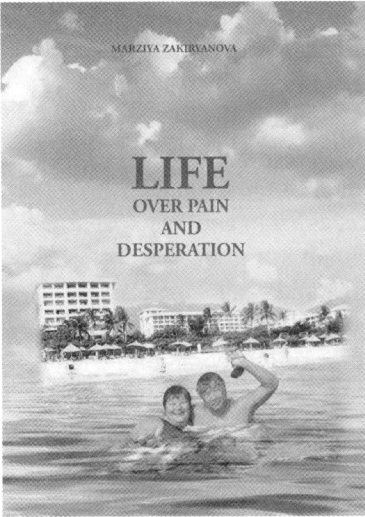

Life over pain and desperation
by Marziya Zakiryanova (2014)

This book was written by someone on the fringe of death. Her life had been split in two: before and after the first day of August 1991 when she, a mother of two small children and full of hopes and plans for the future, became disabled in a single twist of fate. Narrating her tale of self-conquest, the author speaks about how she managed to hold her family together, win the respect and recognition of people around her and above all, protect the fragile concept of 'love' from fortune's cruel turns. By the time the book was submitted to print, Marziya Zakiryanova had passed away. She died after making the last correction to her script. We bid farewell to this remarkable and powerfully creative woman.

HARD BACK
ISBN: **978-0-99278733-2**
RRP: **£14.95**
AVAILABLE ON **KINDLE**

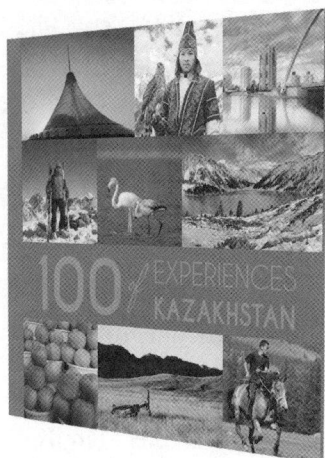

100 experiences of Kazakhstan
by Vitaly Shuptar, Nick Rowan
and Dagmar Schreiber (2014)

The original land of the nomads,
landlocked Kazakhstan and its expansive
steppes present an intriguing border
between Europe and Asia. Dispel
the notion of oil barons and Borat and be
prepared for a warm welcome into a land
full of contrasts. A visit to this newly
independent country will transport you
to a bygone era to discover a country
full of legends and wonders. Whether
searching for the descendants of Genghis Khan - who left his mark on this
land seven hundred years ago - or looking to discover the futuristic
architecture of its capital Astana, visitors cannot fail but be impressed
by what they experience. For those seeking adventure, the formidable Altai
and Tien Shan mountains provide challenges for novices and experts alike

ISBN: 978-0-992787356
RRP: £19.95

Dance of Devils , Jinlar Bazmi
by AbdulhamidIsmoil
and Hamid Ismailov
(Uzbek language),
E-book (2012)

'Dance of Devils' is a novel about the life of a great Uzbek writer Abdulla Qadyri (incidentally, 'Dance of Devils' is the name of one of his earliest short stories). In 1937, Qadyri was going to write a novel, which he said was to make his readers to stop reading his iconic novels "Days Bygone" and "Scorpion from the altar," so beautiful it would have been. The novel would've told about a certain maid, who became a wife of three Khans - a kind of Uzbek Helen of Troy. He told everyone: "I will sit down this winter and finish this novel - I have done my preparatory work, it remains only to write. Then people will stop reading my previous books". He began writing this novel, but on the December 31, 1937 he was arrested.

AVAILABLE ON **KINDLE**
ASIN: B009ZBPV2M

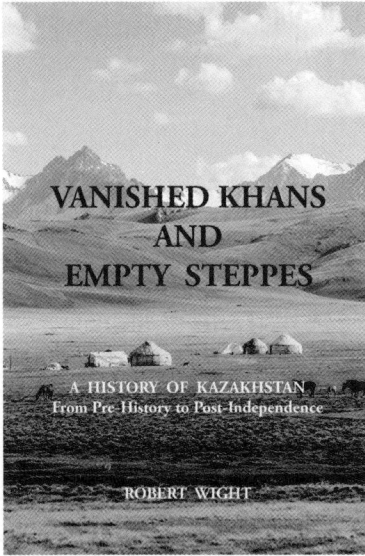

Vanished Khans and Empty Steppes
by Robert Wight (2014)

The book opens with an outline of the history of Almaty, from its nineteenth-century origins as a remote outpost of the Russian empire, up to its present status as the thriving second city of modern-day Kazakhstan. The story then goes back to the Neolithic and early Bronze Ages, and the sensational discovery of the famous Golden Man of the Scythian empire. The transition has been difficult and tumultuous for millions of people, but Vanished Khans and Empty Steppes illustrates how Kazakhstan has emerged as one of the world's most successful post-communist countries.

HARD BACK
ISBN: **978-0-9930444-0-3**
RRP: **£24.95**

PAPERBACK
ISBSN: **978-1-910886-05-2**
RRP: **£14.50**
AVAILABLE ON **KINDLE**

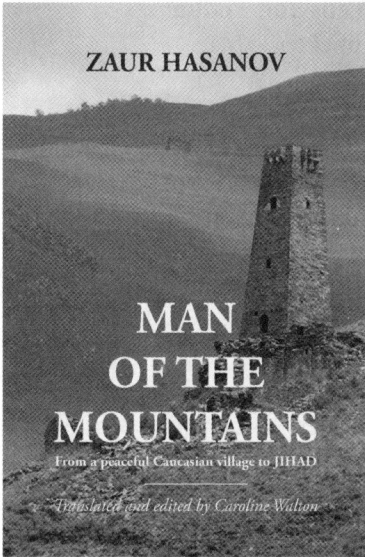

Man of the Mountains
by Abudlla Isa (2014)
(OCABF 2013 Winner)

ZAUR HASANOV

MAN
OF THE
MOUNTAINS
From a peaceful Caucasian village to JIHAD

Translated and edited by Caroline Walton

Man of the Mountains" is a book about a young Muslim Chechen boy, Zaur who becomes a central figure representing the fight of local indigenous people against both the Russians invading the country and Islamic radicals trying to take a leverage of the situation, using it to push their narrow political agenda on the eve of collapse of the USSR. After 9/11 and the invasion of Iraq and Afghanistan by coalition forces, the subject of the Islamic jihadi movement has become an important subject for the Western readers. But few know about the resistance movement from the local intellectuals and moderates against radical Islamists taking strong hold in the area.

PAPERBACK
ISBN: **978-0-9930444-5-8**
RRP: **£14.95**
AVAILABLE ON **KINDLE**

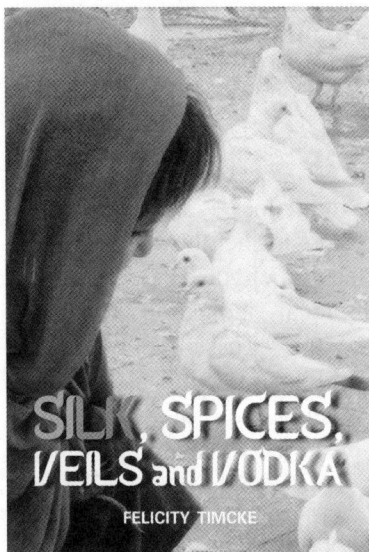

Silk, Spice, Veils and Vodka
by Felicity Timcke (2014)

Felicity Timcke's missive publication, "Silk, Spices, Veils and Vodka" brings both a refreshing and new approach to life on the expat trail. South African by origin, Timcke has lived in some very exotic places, mostly along the more challenging countries of the Silk Road. Although the book's content, which is entirely composed of letters to the author's friends and family, is directed primarily at this group, it provides "20 years of musings" that will enthral and delight those who have either experienced a similar expatriate existence or who are nervously about to depart for one.

PAPERBACK
ISBN: **978-0992787318**
RRP: **£12.50**
AVAILABLE ON **KINDLE**

Finding the Holy Path
by Shahsanem Murray (2014)

"Murray's first book provides an enticing and novel link between her adopted home town of Edinburgh and her origins form Central Asia. Beginning with an investigation into a mysterious lamp that turns up in an antiques shop in Edinburgh, and is bought on impulse, we are quickly brought to the fertile Ferghana valley in Uzbekistan to witness the birth of Kara-Choro, and the start of an enthralling story that links past and present. Told through a vivid and passionate dialogue, this is a tale of parallel discovery and intrigue. The beautifully translated text, interspersed by regional poetry, cannot fail to impress any reader, especially those new to the region who will be affectionately drawn into its heart in this page-turning cultural thriller."

В поисках святого перевала – удивительный приключенческий роман, основанный на исторических источниках. Произведение Мюррей – это временной мостик между эпохами, который помогает нам переместиться в прошлое и уносит нас далеко в 16 век. Закрученный сюжет предоставляет нам уникальную возможность, познакомиться с историейи культурой Центральной Азии. «Первая книга Мюррей предлагает заманчивый роман, связывающий между её приемным городом Эдинбургом и Центральной Азией, откуда настоящее происхождение автора.

RUS ISBN: **978-0-9930444-8-9**
ENGL ISBN: **978-0992787394**
PAPERBACK
RRP: **£12.50**

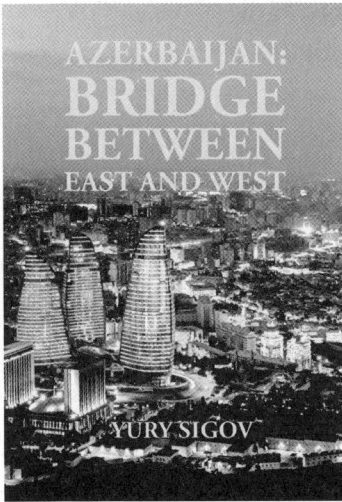

Azerbaijan:
Bridge between East and West
by Yury Sigov, 2015

Azerbaijan: Bridge between East and West, Yury Sigov narrates a comprehensive and compelling story about Azerbaijan. He balances the country's rich cultural heritage, wonderful people and vibrant environment with its modern political and economic strategies. Readers will get the chance to thoroughly explore Azerbaijan from many different perspectives and discover a plethora of innovations and idea, including the recipe for Azerbaijan's success as a nation and its strategies for the future. The book also explores the history of relationships between United Kingdom and Azerbaijan.

HARD BACK
ISBN: **978-0-9930444-9-6**
RRP: **£24.50**
AVAILABLE ON **KINDLE**

Kashmir Song
by Sharaf Rashidov
(translation by Alexey Ulko, OCABF 2014 Winner). 2015

This beautiful illustrated novella offers a sensitive reworking of an ancient and enchanting folk story which although rooted in Kashmir is, by nature of its theme, universal in its appeal.

Alternative interpretations of this tale are explored by Alexey Ulko in his introduction, with references to both politics and contemporary literature, and the author's epilogue further reiterates its philosophical dimension.

The Kashmir Song is a timeless tale, which true to the tradition of classical folklore, can be enjoyed on a number of levels by readers of all ages.

COMING SOON!!!
ISBN: 978-0-9930444-2-7
RRP: £29.50

Land of forty tribes
by Farideh Heyat, 2015

Sima Omid, a British-Iranian anthropologist in search of her Turkic roots, takes on a university teaching post in Kyrgyzstan. It is the year following 9/11, when the US is asserting its influence in the region. Disillusioned with her long-standing relationship, Sima is looking for a new man in her life. But the foreign men she meets are mostly involved in relationships with local women half their age, and the Central Asian men she finds highly male chauvinist and aggressive towards women.

PAPERBACK
ISBN: **978-0-9930444-4-1**
RRP: **£14.95**

Terror: events, facts, evidence.
by Eldar Samadov, 2015

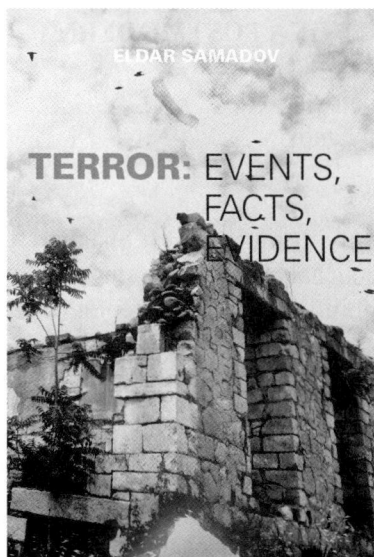

This book is based on research carried out since 1988 on territorial claims of Armenia against Azerbaijan, which led to the escalation of the conflict over Nagorno-Karabakh. This escalation included acts of terror by Armenian terrorist and other armed gangs not only in areas where intensive armed confrontations took place but also away from the fighting zones. This book, not for the first time, reflects upon the results of numerous acts of premeditated murder, robbery, armed attack and other crimes through collected material related to criminal cases which have been opened at various stages following such crimes. The book is meant for political scientists, historians, lawyers, diplomats and a broader audience.

PAPERBACK
ISBN: **978-1-910886-00-7**
RRP: **£9.99**
AVAILABLE ON **KINDLE**

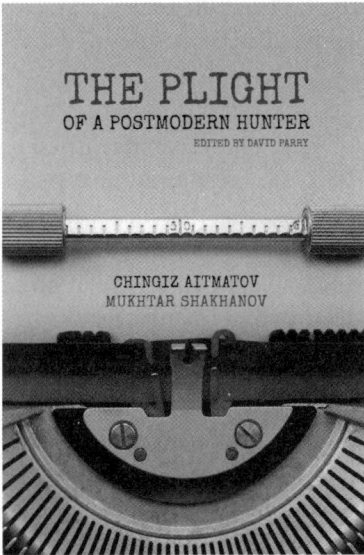

THE PLIGHT OF A POSTMODERN HUNTER

Chlngiz Aitmatov.
Mukhtar Shakhanov
(2015)

"Delusion of civilization" by M. Shakhanov is an epochal poem, rich in prudence and nobility – as is his foremother steppe. It is the voice of the Earth, which raised itself in defense of the human soul. This is a new genre of spiritual ecology. As such, this book is written from the heart of a former tractor driver, who knows all the "scars and wrinkles" of the soil - its thirst for human intimacy. This book is also authored from the perspective of an outstanding intellectual whose love for national traditions has grown as universal as our common great motherland.

I dare say, this book is a spiritual instrument of patriotism for all humankind. Hence, there is something gentle, kind, and sad, about the old swan-song of Mukhtar's brave ancestors. Those who for six months fought to the death to protect Grand Otrar - famous worldwide for its philosophers and rich library, from the hordes of Genghis Khan.

HARDBACK
LANGUAGES ENG
ISBN: **978-1-910886-11-3**
RRP: **£17.50**

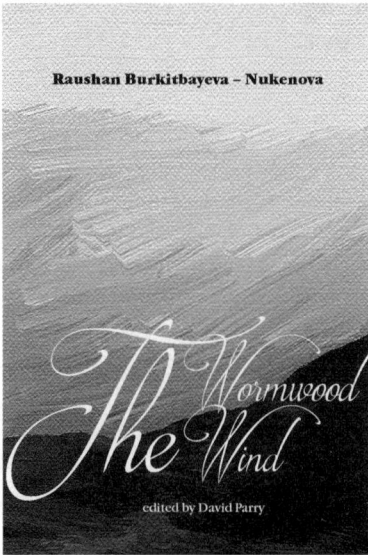

The Wormwood Wind
Raushan
Burkitbayeva- Nukenova (2015)

A single unstated assertion runs throughout The Wormwood Wind, arguing,
amid its lyrical nooks and crannies, we
are only fully human when our imagina-
tions are free. Possibly this is the primary
glittering insight behind Nukenova's col-
laboration with hidden Restorative Pow-
ers above her pen. No one would doubt,
for example, when she hints that the moment schoolchildren read about their surrounding environment they are acting
in a healthy and developmental manner.
Likewise, when she implies any adult who has the courage to think "outside
the box" quickly gains a reputation for adaptability in their private affairs –
hardly anyone would doubt her. General affirmations demonstrating this sublime and liberating contribution to Global Text will prove dangerous to un-
wary readers, while its intoxicating rhythms and rhymes will lead a grateful
few to elative revolutions inside their own souls. Thus, I unreservedly recom-
mend this ingenious work to Western readers.

HARD BACK
LANGUAGES ENG
ISBN: **978-1-910886-12-0**
RRP: **£14.95**

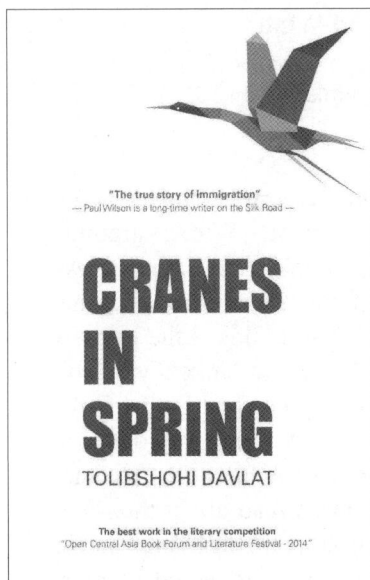

"Cranes in Spring"
by Tolibshohi Davlat
(2015)

"The true story of immigration"
— Paul Wilson is a long-time writer on the Silk Road —

CRANES IN SPRING
TOLIBSHOHI DAVLAT

The best work in the literary competition
"Open Central Asia Book Forum and Literature Festival - 2014"

This novel highlights a complex issue that millions of Tajiks face when becoming working migrants in Russia due to lack of opportunities at home. Fresh out of school, Saidakbar decides to go to Russia as he hopes to earn money to pay for his university tuition. His parents reluctantly let him go providing he is accompanied by his uncle, Mustakim, an experienced migrant. And so begins this tale of adventure and heartache that reflects the reality of life faced by many Central Asian migrants. Mistreatment, harassment and backstabbing join the Tajik migrants as they try to pull through in a foreign country. Davlat vividly narrates the brutality of the law enforcement officers but also draws attention to kindness and help of several ordinary people in Russia. How will Mustakim and Saidakbar's journey end? Intrigued by the story starting from the first page, one cannot put the book down until it's finished.

COMING SOON

LANGUAGES ENG / RUS
HARDBACK
ISBN: **978-1-910886-06-9**

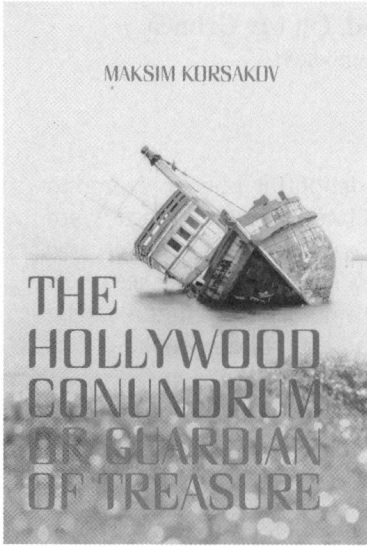

**The Hollywood Conundrum
or Guardian of Treasure**
Maksim Korsakov
(2015)

In this groundbreaking experimental novella, Maxim Korsakov breaks all the preconceived rules of genre and literary convention to deliver a work rich in humour, style, and fantasy. Starting with a so-called "biographical" account of the horrors lurking beneath marriages of convenience and the self-delusions necessary to maintain these relationships, he then speedily moves to a screenplay, which would put most James Bond movies to shame. As if international espionage were not enough, the author teases his readers with lost treasure maps, revived Khanates, sports car jousting, ancient aliens who possess the very secrets of immortality, and the lineal descendants of legendary Genghis Khan. All in all, an ingenious book, as well as s clear critique of traditional English narrative convention.

LANGUAGES ENG / RUS
PAPERBACK
ISBN: **978-1-910886-14-4**
RRP: **£24.95**

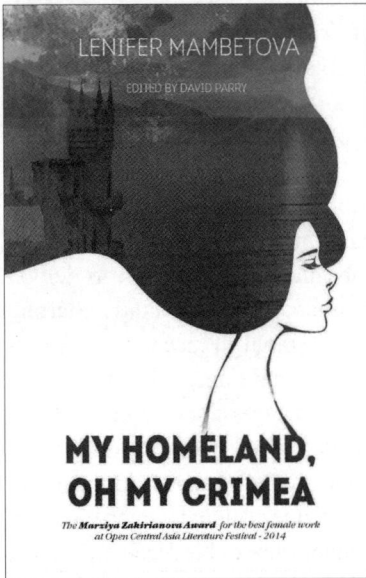

My Homeland, Oh My Crimea
by Lenifer Mambetova
(2015)

Mambetova's delightful poems, exploring the hopes and fates of Crimean Tartars, are a timely and evocative reminder of how deep a people's roots can be, but also how adaptable and embracing foreigners can be of their adopted country, its people and its traditions.

COMING SOON
LANGUAGES ENG / RUS
HARDBACK
ISBN: **978-1-910886-04-5**